"I Can't Marry You," She Protested.

"Can't?"

"You said it yourself," she accused. "I don't belong here, Latif. It's not my home."

"A woman belongs with her husband. His home is her home. You belong with me. You are Bagestani. Your blood is here. Your heart is here. Your people call to you. I call to you."

His hands tightened on her, as if he knew that he had lost. He bent and kissed her again.

"Answer me," he commanded.

"Please take me as a lover," she sobbed, "and don't ask me for more."

"If I love you, I make you mine!"

Her heart twisting with hurt, she drew back from him. But fear was more powerful than the pain. She knew this was not a question of heart, or even of love. This was powerful sexual passion, masquerading as love, and she would be ten times worse than a fool to be swayed by it....

Dear Reader,

Welcome to another stellar month of smart, sensual reads. Our bestselling series DYNASTIES: THE DANFORTHS comes to a compelling conclusion with Leanne Banks's *Shocking the Senator* as honest Abe Danforth finally gets his story. Be sure to look for the start of our next family dynasty story when Eileen Wilks launches DYNASTIES: THE ASHTONS next month and brings you all the romance and intrigue you could ever desire...all set in the fabulous Napa Valley.

Award-winning author Jennifer Greene is back this month to conclude THE SCENT OF LAVENDER series with the astounding *Wild in the Moment*. And just as the year brings some things to a close, new excitement blossoms as Alexandra Sellers gives us the next installment of her SONS OF THE DESERT series with *The Ice Maiden's Sheikh*. The always-enjoyable Emilie Rose will wow you with her tale of *Forbidden Passion*—let's just say the book starts with a sexy tryst on a staircase. We'll let you imagine the rest. Brenda Jackson is also back this month with her unforgettable hero Storm Westmoreland, in *Riding the Storm*. (A title that should make you go hmmm.) And rounding things out is up-and-coming author Michelle Celmer's second book, *The Seduction Request*.

I would love to hear what you think about Silhouette Desire, so please feel free to drop me a line c/o Silhouette Books, 233 Broadway, Suite 1001, New York, NY 10279. Let me know what miniseries you are enjoying, your favorite authors and things you would like to see in the future.

With thanks,

Melissa Jeglinski

Melissa Jeglinski
Senior Editor
Silhouette Desire

Please address questions and book requests to:
Silhouette Reader Service
U.S.: 3010 Walden Ave., P.O. Box 1325, Buffalo, NY 14269
Canadian: P.O. Box 609, Fort Erie, Ont. L2A 5X3

THE ICE MAIDEN'S
SHEIKH

ALEXANDRA SELLERS

Silhouette®

Desire

Published by Silhouette Books

America's Publisher of Contemporary Romance

SILHOUETTE BOOKS

ISBN 0-373-76623-8

THE ICE MAIDEN'S SHEIKH

Books by Alexandra Sellers

ALEXANDRA SELLERS

is the author of over twenty-five novels and a feline language text published in 1997 and still selling.

Born and raised in Canada, Alexandra first came to London as a drama student. Now she lives near Hampstead Heath with her husband, Nick. They share housekeeping with Monsieur, who jumped through the window one day and announced, as cats do, that he was moving in.

What she would miss most on a desert island is shared laughter.

Readers can write to Alexandra at P.O. Box 9449, London NW3 2WH, UK, England.

One

The bride was missing.

Jalia ran along the balcony, anxiety beating in her temples. The soft green silk of the bridesmaid's veil fell forward yet again to cover her face, half blinding her, adding to the helpless confusion she felt. But she had no time now to struggle with it.

What was wrong? Where had Noor gone, and why?

Oh, please let it be just one of her games. Let her not have changed her mind like this, in the most embarrassing possible way....

"Noor!" she called softly. "Noor, where are you?"

A confused, murmuring silence was replacing the earlier sounds of celebration coming from the large central courtyard of the palatial house, and Jalia's heart sank. Hopeless now to think she might find

Noor quickly so that the wedding could proceed without an obvious delay.

This balcony overlooked a smaller courtyard. If Noor had come out here, surely she would have realized at once that she had gone the wrong way?

''Noor?'' She leaned over the railing. Below, the courtyard was empty. A fountain played with the sunlight, creating an endless spray of diamonds; flowers danced in the breeze; but no human shadow moved across the beautiful tiles.

Ahead of her, in a breathtaking series of arches and columns, stretched the shadowed balcony, leading to an ancient arched door like the secret door of childhood dreams. No one.

''Noor?'' A bead of sweat dropped from under the veil onto her hand. Half heat, half nerves. Was the bride's flight her—Jalia's—fault? People would think so. Jalia would be blamed, by some more fiercely than by others.

Latif Abd al Razzaq Shahin, for one, would condemn Jalia's interference in her cousin's sudden engagement to his friend Bari. He already had, and Jalia was still smarting from the contact.

''Noor!'' she cried more loudly, because secrecy was impossible now. Oh, how like Noor to create a melodramatic, self-centred, eleventh-hour panic, instead of taking the calm, rational course Jalia had advised. All the princess bride had had to do was insist on taking a little more time before committing herself irrevocably to a stranger in a strange land!

And how like Noor, too, to leave her cousin to pick up the pieces. Thanks to Noor's open-mouth policy, Jalia's opposition to the hasty wedding was well-known in the family. People would blame her for this outcome.

He would blame her. Not that she cared a damn for Latif Abd al Razzaq's opinion, but his criticism could be biting and cruel, and he disliked Jalia almost as much as she disliked him. He would probably relish this opportunity to put her so drastically in the wrong.

As if the thought had given rise to the devil—or the devil to the thought?—the man himself appeared before her on the balcony a few yards away. He was wearing the magnificent ceremonial costume of a Cup Companion, but she shivered as if at the approach of menace and dodged behind one of the columns of worn, sand-coloured brick.

But she had been mesmerized a second too long, and he struck fast, like the falcon he was named for. The next moment he was before her, blocking her path.

"Where has your cousin gone?" demanded Latif Abd al Razzaq Shahin, Cup Companion to the new Sultan, in a commanding voice.

Jalia's skin twitched all the way to her scalp. She shrank against the pillar in instinctive animal alarm, then forced herself to stand straight. Her face was totally covered. How could he know who she was, behind the veil? He was only guessing.

"I dant now vot you are tawkeen abowt," she said in a deep, breathy voice. "You are made a meestek."

He shook his head with the unconscious, bone-deep arrogance she so hated. Whatever Latif Abd al Razzaq decided to own was his, whatever he decided to do was right, and everyone else—life itself—had to submit. That was the message.

Anger sang through her blood and nerves. How she detested the man! He was everything she most disliked about the East.

"The game is over, Jalia," he said through his teeth. "Where did she go?"

She wanted to walk away, but her path was blocked by his body. She would have to push past him, and she discovered that she was deeply reluctant to do so.

"I am not who you sink. Lit me pess," she commanded, with icy disdain.

He raised a hand, his teeth flashing as she instinctively flinched. Slowly and deliberately he caught a corner of the scarf that covered her to draw it back over her head.

Her thick, ash-coloured hair lay over one side of her face, a heavy wave curving in against the high, delicate cheek, half masking one slate-green eye as she lifted her chin with a cool, haughty look.

His hand remained tangled in the scarf, the pale hair brushing his knuckles as Latif and the Princess gazed at each other. Deep mutual hostility seemed to warp the air between them.

After a curious, frozen moment, his fingers released the supple silk and his hand withdrew. With the breaking of the connection the air could move again.

"Where has your cousin gone?" he asked in a harsh, low voice.

Her chin went up another notch, and her jade eyes flashed cool fire. She showed no embarrassment at having been caught in a lie.

"Don't speak to me in that tone of voice, Excellency."

"Where?"

"I have no idea where Noor is. Perhaps in a bathroom somewhere, being sick. I am looking for her. You waste time by keeping me here. Let me pass, please."

"If you are looking for her in the house, it is you who waste time. She has fled."

Jalia's heart dropped like a diving seabird. "*Fled?* I don't believe you! Fled where?"

"That is the question Bari sent me to ask you. Where has the Princess gone?"

"Are you telling me she's left the house?"

"Don't you know it?"

Involuntarily she glanced down at her own closed fist. "No! How would I know? I was waiting with the other bridesmaids...."

His eyes followed hers. Her fist was clenched tight on something. In a move that was almost possessive, his hand closed on her wrist. Calmly he forced her hand over, so that the fingertips were uppermost.

"What is it?" His eyes flicked from her hand to her face and rested there, with a grimly determined look.

"None of your bloody business! Let go of me!"

"Open your hand, Princess Jalia."

She struggled, but his strength was firmly turned against her now, and she could not get free. After a moment in which they stared at each other, she had the humiliation of feeling the pressure of his finger between her knuckles, forcing her hand open.

On her open palm a diamond solitaire glittered with painful brilliance.

Again his green eyes moved to her face, and the expression she saw in them made her stiffen.

"What is this?" he demanded as, with long, strong fingers, he ignored her struggles and plucked the ring from her palm. He let her wrist go so suddenly she staggered.

He held it up in a shaft of sunlight that found its way into the shadows of the balcony through some chink in the ancient arched roof. It glowed and flashed, but even the fabulous al Khalid Diamond couldn't match Latif Abd al Razzaq's eyes for glitter.

"What is this?" he repeated accusingly.

"A cheap imitation?" Jalia drawled with exaggerated irony, because Noor's engagement diamond was unmistakable. The al Khalid Diamond was probably worth about a thousand times what had been paid for the modest engagement band of opals encircling Jalia's own finger.

The ring's value, as much as its stark, flashing beauty, had delighted Noor, but it didn't tempt Jalia one bit. She knew too well what came with a ring like that—a man like Bari al Khalid...or Latif Abd al Razzaq.

"Tell me where your cousin has gone."

"What makes you so damned sure *I* know? Back to the palace, I suppose! Where else would she go?"

Her scarf was slipping forward over her face again. Jalia began irritably tearing at the pins that held it. What a stupid bloody custom it was, the bride having to be chosen from among a group of bridesmaids, all with scarves draped over their heads, to test the groom's perspicacity! Everyone knew the groom was always tipped off as to exactly what his bride would be wearing, and today anyway Noor had infuriated all the diehards by wearing Western white. Bari would have had to be blind and ignorant to miss her, even under the yards of enveloping tulle.

But everyone had insisted on playing the ancient ritual out, nevertheless. It was just one of many reasons why Jalia was grateful that her parents had fled Bagestan years before she was born, and why she was not happy about their plans for coming back.

Latif Abd al Razzaq was another.

He gazed at her, incredulous. Jalia knew he would never believe that, as opposed as she had been to Noor's hasty, ill-conceived wedding, Jalia had had absolutely nothing to do with this last-minute sabotage.

But what did she care? What Latif Abd al Razzaq thought of her mattered precisely nothing to her.

She flung the beautifully embroidered scarf away from her, not caring that it caught on a rosebush bristling with thorns.

"You have her ring."

"Yes," Jalia admitted coolly.

"How did you get it?"

"What makes it your business to ask me that question, Excellency? And in that particular tone of voice?"

His voice shifted to a deep growl. "What tone of voice do you want from me, Princess?" he asked abruptly.

Jalia's skin twitched, but she brushed aside her nervous discomfort.

"I would be quite happy never to hear your voice at all."

Jalia was glad of Latif Abd al Razzaq's dislike, of the fierce disapproval that he didn't bother to hide. A man like him could only be an enemy—she knew that much—and it was safer to have the enmity in the open. Then no one was fooled.

Looking up at him now, in the deep green silk jacket that intensified the dangerous depths of his emerald eyes, a thickly ornamented ceremonial sword slung from one hip, she felt the antipathy like a powerful current between them.

She didn't know why he should dislike her, though she understood her own deep dislike of him clearly enough: he embodied everything she least liked in a man. Autocratic, overbearing, sure of himself, super-masculine, proud of it.

"Did Noor speak to you before she fled?"

She sighed her outrage. "What do you hope to gain by this?"

"Did she drop any hint? Did she say she was heading to the palace?"

"Will you stop imagining I stage-managed this? Whatever Noor is doing, and whoever is helping her, I had nothing to do with it! Has it occurred to you *at all* that this may not be what it looks like? For all you or I know, Noor was enticed out of the house by some threat—"

"Ah! She did not leave of her own accord?" The emerald eyes glinted with mocking admiration.

"I don't know! Can't you get it past your rigid mind-set that I have no idea why Noor has left—if she has?"

"If?"

"Well, I only have your word for it, Excellency, and you have now and then shown a predisposition to wanting to see me put in the wrong!"

His Excellency gazed at her without speaking for a moment.

"We must talk to the others. Come."

He turned on his heel and started along the wide, roofed terrace, then entered the arched passageway that led into the main courtyard of the house.

Jalia's jaw clenched, but she had to talk to Noor's parents, and that meant apparently obeying Latif's command. Besides, she reminded herself, he had the ring, and if she wasn't present he would be sure to put some damning interpretation on the fact that he had found it in Jalia's own hand.

Two

They descended the magnificent worn marble staircase to the main courtyard, where an air of subdued confusion hung over the wedding party. People were milling around, wondering and speculating, or simply looking bewildered.

Only the Sultan and Sultana looked unruffled, serenely chatting to whoever approached them, so that a tiny island of calm was created in the sea of unhappy excitement.

"What happened?"

"Where is the Princess?"

"Has someone been taken ill?"

"Is the wedding called off?"

The cloud of questions billowed her way, but Jalia didn't stop; Latif was striding along as though the people were so many trees, and she was grateful to have the excuse to keep going. She had nothing to tell.

In the spacious, pillared reception hall, the families were grouped together on the low platform at one end of the room, talking in quiet, distressed voices. Everywhere the rich carpets were spread with tablecloths laid with china, crystal and silver, as if a thousand people had decided to picnic at once.

"Jalia!" Her mother and aunt, both looking tearful and confused, ran to her. "Did she say anything to you before she went? Where is she going? What happened?"

"H-has she really left the house?" Jalia stammered. She had never seen the two princesses so deeply distressed. Oh, how she wished she had been a little more reasoned in her opposition to Noor's wedding! If her interference had contributed to this unhappiness...

"Didn't you know? She has gone! She took the limousine! Still wearing her dress and veil!"

"She didn't even change?" Jalia gasped. "But where could she go in her dress and veil, except back to the palace? Did she take any luggage?"

"The servants say it is all still stacked in the forecourt, nothing taken. There's no sign of her at the palace. They will phone if she turns up, but if she had been heading there, surely she would have arrived by now! Tell us what happened!" her aunt begged.

"Aunt, I have no idea what happened! I wasn't with her."

But any information, she knew, was better than nothing at a time like this. "I went up with the other bridesmaids to collect her at the right time. The hairdresser said she'd gone into the bathroom. We waited. After about five minutes, I followed her in. She wasn't there.

"I'm sorry, Aunt Zaynab, I should have raised the alarm right away, but I thought it was just nerves or she'd gone out to the wrong balcony or—" She bit her lip. "So I went to look for her. I suppose that wasted time, but I thought..."

Her aunt patted her hand. "Yes, you thought it was just one of Noor's little games, Jalia. Anyone would have. But it's more serious than that. It must be, for her to leave the house. Did she say anything to anyone? When I was with her she was fine, laughing, so happy and excited...."

"Aunt, she—I found her ring. It was on the floor in the room I am using. She must have gone out that way to avoid being seen."

Latif produced the al Khalid Diamond. Her aunt all but snatched it from him, moaning with horror.

"She must have panicked," someone offered. "Bridal jitters."

All around the room, eyes dark with blame rested on Jalia. She was saved from whatever might have been said next when Bari al Khalid's uncle came into the room, looking harassed and bewildered.

"Bari has gone, too! The guards say he drove out a few minutes after Noor!"

"*Barakullah!*" Princess Zaynab wailed. "What is going on?"

Latif Abd al Razzaq spoke, his calm voice stilling the rustle of horrified panic. "One of the guards saw her drive away and came to tell Bari. He went after her to bring her back."

Where Latif stood was suddenly the centre of the room. Everyone turned to gaze at him.

"He asked me to find Jalia and ask her what she knew."

Again, as one, they all turned more or less accusing eyes on Jalia.

"I don't know anything about it!" she wailed. "She didn't say a word to me." She flicked a glance at Latif. She was sure he had deliberately dropped her in it. "Is it possible she got a phone call—?"

"The maids say not." Princess Muna answered her daughter.

"Where's her mobile? Did she phone someone?"

"In her handbag, in the bedroom. She didn't even take money, Jalia!"

"Oh, my daughter! What is to be done now?" Princess Zaynab cried. "If Bari finds her, so angry as he must be…"

"I will go after them," Latif announced.

"Ah, Your Excellency, thank you! But if you find Noor—"

"Jalia will come with me."

Jalia looked up in startled indignation. "Me? What good can—"

Her mother hurried into the breach. "Yes, go with His Excellency, Jalia. You might be able to help."

Go with Latif Abd al Razzaq? The words had a kind of premonitory electricity that made her skin shiver into gooseflesh. Why was he asking for her company, when he clearly thought her poison?

"Help how? I don't know where she's gone!" she protested, but not one face relaxed. She glared at Latif. "I have absolutely no idea what she's…"

He only lifted an eyebrow, but it was a comment that she was protesting too much. She could see in their faces that most people saw his point. Damn the man!

"Of course you don't, Jalia," Princess Zaynab murmured, patting her hand again, her soft dark eyes liquid with worry. "But Bari will be so angry. Please go with Latif. She may be…calm her down and bring her back. Tell her it's not too late. We will wait here."

Outside, a hot, dry wind smacked her, blowing her wedding finery against her body and dust into her eyes.

The hem of her flowing skirt and the bodice of her tunic were encrusted with gold embroidery, sequins and gold coins. How stupid to go searching for Noor dressed like this! As if she were one of the mountain tribeswomen she had seen in the bazaar, who even seemed to go shopping dressed in magnificently decorated clothes. Some of them were blond, with green eyes, like Jalia, though she had always believed that her own colouring came from her French grandmother.

By the time Latif's car arrived from the parking area, her skin was glowing with sweat and she realized she had taken nothing to protect herself from the sun.

The Cup Companion's ceremonial sword in its jewelled scabbard had been tossed into the back seat. He watched her silently as she slipped into the seat beside him.

"I can't imagine why you feel you need me!" she remarked.

Sheikh Latif Abd al Razzaq gave her a long unreadable look.

"Need you?" he repeated with arrogant disdain, and she felt a strange, dry heat from him, like invisible fire deep under dry grass that hadn't yet burst into open flame. "I was getting you out of the way before they all turned on you. Not that you don't richly deserve it."

As the big gates opened the car crept forward, and two men and a woman flung themselves towards it. One man had a camera on his shoulder, and the woman was thrusting a tape recorder towards Latif's face as she banged on the window.

"Excellency, may we have a word, please?"

"Can you tell us what happened? Did the wedding take place?"

"Why did Princess Noor drive off?"

More reporters were now surging around the car, forcing Latif to drive very slowly to avoid running them down. The questions continued nonstop, shouted through the windows at them, while rapid-fire flashes burst against the glass. Several little red eyes gazed hotly into the car, as if the cameras themselves took a fevered interest in the occupants.

"Damn, oh damn!" Jalia cried.

"Don't give them an opening," he advised flatly.

Jalia had to admire Latif's cool. Although forced to drive at a speed of inches per hour, he gave no sign that he heard or saw the media people. She, meanwhile, found her temper rising as the reporters deliberately blocked their path, banging on the car as if somehow they might not have been noticed.

The fact that the air-conditioning hadn't kicked in and the car was like an oven didn't help her mood.

"Princess! Your Highness!" someone called, and she turned in dismay as another flash went off right in her face. How did they know? She had been so careful!

"Can you tell us why Noor ran?"

"Where did she go?"

"Was she escaping a forced marriage, Princess?"

Forced? Noor had been laughing all the way to the altar. Jalia couldn't prevent a slight outraged shake of her head. Instantly someone leaped on this sign.

"The marriage was her own free choice? Are you surprised by the turn of events?"

But she had learned her lesson, and stared straight ahead. "Damn, damn, damn!" she muttered.

Latif put his foot down on both brake and gas, spinning the tires on the unpaved road. Immediately the car was enveloped in a cloud of dust that blinded the cameras.

Coughing, frantically waving their hands in front of their noses, the journalists backed away. Latif lifted his foot off the brake and, belching dust, the car spurted away.

For a moment they laughed together, like children who have escaped tyranny. Jalia flicked Latif a look of half-grudging admiration. She would have congratulated anyone else, but with Latif there was an ever-present constraint.

"I've been so careful to avoid being identified!" she wailed. "How did they know who I was?"

Unlike Noor, who had reacted with delight, Jalia

had greeted the news that she was a princess of Bagestan with reticence, and was determined to avoid any public discovery of the fact. She hadn't told even her close friends back home.

Who could have given her away, and why?

Latif's dark gaze flicked her and she twitched in a kind of animal alarm. It was just the effect he had on her; there was no reason for it. But it annoyed her, every time.

"They just took an educated guess, probably. Your reaction gave you away."

The truth of that was instantly obvious.

"Oh, *damn* it!" cried Jalia. "Why did I ever take off my veil?"

Three

Laughter burst from his throat, a roar of amusement that made the windows ring. But it wasn't friendly amusement, she knew. He was laughing at her.

"Does it matter so much—a photo in a few papers?"

Jalia shrugged irritably. "You're a Cup Companion—the press attention is part of your job. And anyway, you're one of twelve. I'm a university lecturer in a small city in Scotland, where princesses are not numbered in the dozens. I don't want anyone at home to know."

He slowed at the approach to the paved road and turned the car towards the city. Two journalists' cars were now following them.

"Aren't you exaggerating? You aren't a member

of the British royal family, after all. Just a small Middle Eastern state.''

''I hope you're right.'' She chewed her lip. ''But the media in Europe have had an ongoing obsession with the royal family of the Barakat Emirates for the past five years—and it jumped to Bagestan like wildfire over a ditch the moment Ghasib's dictatorship fell and Ashraf al Jawadi was crowned. If I'm outed as a princess of Bagestan, my privacy is—'' Blowing a small raspberry she made a sign of cutting her throat.

''Only if you continue to live abroad,'' he pointed out. ''Why not come home?''

Jalia stiffened. ''Because Bagestan is not 'home' to me,'' she said coldly. ''I am English, as you well know.''

The black gaze flicked her again, unreadable. ''That can be overcome,'' he offered, as if her Englishness were some kind of disability, and Jalia clenched her teeth. ''You would soon fit in. There are many posts available in the universities here. Ash is working hard to—''

''I teach classical Arabic to English speakers, Latif,'' Jalia reminded him dryly. ''I don't even speak Bagestani Arabic.''

She felt a sudden longing for the cool of an English autumn, rain against the windows, the smell of books and cheap carpet and coffee in her tiny university office, the easy, unemotional chatter of her colleagues.

''I am sure you know that educated Bagestani Arabic is close to the classical Quranic language. You would soon pick it up.'' He showed his white teeth in a smile, and her stomach tightened. "The bazaar might take you a little longer."

The big souk in Medinat al Bostan was a clamour on a busy day, and the clash between country and city dialects had over the years spontaneously produced the bazaar's very own dialect, called by everyone *shaerashouk*—"bazaar poetry."

Jalia looked at him steadily, refusing to share the joke. She had heard the argument from her mother too often to laugh now. And his motives were certainly suspect.

"And I'd be even more in the public eye, wouldn't I?" she observed with a wide-eyed, you-don't-fool-me-for-a-minute look.

"Here you would be one of many, and your activities would rarely come under the spotlight unless you wished it. The palace machine would protect you."

"It would also dictate to me," she said coolly. "No, thank you! I prefer independence and anonymity."

He didn't answer, but she saw his jaw clench with suppressed annoyance. For a moment she was on the brink of asking him why it should mean anything to him, but Jalia, too, suppressed the instinct. With Latif Abd al Razzaq, it was better to avoid the personal.

Silence fell between them. Latif concentrated on his driving. One of the press cars passed, a camera trained on them, and then roared off in a cloud of exhaust.

She couldn't stop irritably turning the conversation over in her head. Why was he pushing her? What business was it of Latif Abd al Razzaq's where she lived?

"Why are you carrying my mother's banner?" she demanded after a short struggle. "From her it's just about understandable. What's your angle? Why do you care what I do with my life?"

In the silence that fell, Jalia watched a muscle leap in his jaw. She had the impression that he was struggling for words.

"Do you not care about this country?" he demanded at last, his voice harsh and grating on her. "Bagestan has suffered serious loss to its professional and academic class over the past thirty years—too many educated people fled abroad. If its citizens who were born abroad do not return... You are an al Jawadi by birth, granddaughter of the deposed Sultan. Do you not feel that the al Jawadi should show the way?"

Jalia felt a curious, indefinable sense of letdown.

"You've already convinced my parents to return," she said coolly, for Latif's efforts on their behalf, tracking down titles to her family's expropriated property and tracing lost art treasures grabbed by Ghasib's favourites, had been largely successful, paving the way for them to make the shift.

"And my younger sister is considering it. Why can't you be satisfied with that?"

"Your parents are retirement age. Your sister is a schoolgirl."

Jalia was now feeling the pressure. "Nice to have a captive audience!" she snapped. "Is this why you decided I should come with you on this wild-goose chase? You wanted to deliver a lecture? Do you enjoy preaching duty to people? You should have been a mullah, Latif! Maybe it's not too late even now!"

He flashed her a look. "My opinion would not anger you if you did not, in your heart, accept what I say. It is yourself you are angry with—the part that tells you you have a duty that is larger than your personal life."

She was, oddly, lost for an answer to this ridiculous charge. It simply wasn't true. Neither in her heart nor her head did she feel any obligation to return to Bagestan to nurture its recovery from thirty years of misrule. Until a few weeks ago she hadn't spent one day in the country of her parents' birth—why should she now be expected to treat it as her own homeland?

In spite of her parents' best efforts to prevent it, England was home to her.

"Look—I've got a life to live, and I've paid a price for the choices I've made. Why should I now throw away the sense of belonging I've struggled for all my life, and reach for another to put in its place? I don't belong here, however deeply my parents do. I never will."

He didn't answer, and another long silence fell, during which he watched the road and she gazed out at the vast stretch of desert, thinking.

Her parents had tried to keep her from feeling she belonged in England, the land of her birth, and she was resentfully aware that to some extent they had succeeded. Her sense of place was less rooted than her friends'—she had always known that.

Maybe that was why she clung so firmly to what

she did feel. She knew how difficult it was to find a sense of belonging. Such things didn't come at will.

At the time of the coup some three decades ago, her parents had been newly married. Her mother, one of the daughters of the Sultan's French wife, Sonia, and her father, scion of a tribal chief allied by blood and marriage to the al Jawadi for generations past, had both been in grave danger from Ghasib's squad of assassins. They had fled to Parvan and taken new identities, and the then King of Parvan, Kavad Panj, had put the couple on the staff of the Parvan Embassy in London.

Jalia had passed her childhood in a country that was not "her own," raised on dreams of the land that was. As she grew older, she began to fear the power of those dreams that gripped her parents so inescapably, and to resent that distant homeland from which she was forever banished. From a child who had thrived on the tales of another landscape, another people, another way of being, she had grown into a sceptical, wary teenager determined to avoid the trap her parents had set for her.

When she turned sixteen they had told her the great secret of their lives—they were not ordinary Bagestani exiles, but members of the royal family. Sultan Hafzuddin, the deposed monarch who had figured so largely in her bedtime stories, was her own grandfather.

Jalia had been sworn to secrecy, but the torch had to be passed to her hands: one day the monarchy would be restored, and if her parents did not live to see that day, Jalia must go to the new Sultan....

Her parents had lived to see the day. And now Jalia's life was threatened with total disruption. Her parents, thrilled to join the great Return, were urgent that their elder daughter should do the same. But Jalia knew that in Bagestan something mysterious and powerful threatened her, the thing that had obsessed her parents from her earliest memories.

And she did not want to foster the empty dream that she ''belonged'' in an alien land that she neither knew nor understood. That way lay lifelong unhappiness.

Attending the Coronation had been an inescapable necessity, but it had been a brief visit, no more—until her foolish cousin Noor had undertaken to fall madly in lust with Bari al Khalid, one of the Sultan's new Cup Companions, and promised to marry him.

''Showing the way for us all!'' Jalia's mother declared, wiping from her eye a tear which in no way clouded its beady gaze on her elder daughter.

Her mother had been convinced then that Jalia had only to flutter her lashes to similarly knock Latif Abd al Razzaq to his knees, and was almost desperate for her daughter to make the attempt.

Princess Muna had wasted no time in checking out the handsome Cup Companion's marital status and background: not merely the Sultan's Cup Companion, but since the death of his father two years ago, the leader of his tribe.

''He's called the *Shahin,* Jalia. No one's sure whether the word is an ancient word for king or really does mean *falcon,* as the myth says, but the holder of that title is traditionally one of the most respected voices on the Tribal Council. Not that Ghasib ever consulted the council, but the Sultan will.''

Although Jalia hadn't believed for a minute that the fierce-eyed sheikh was attracted to her, the mere thought of what complications would ensue if he or any Bagestani should declare himself had terrified her. She had gone home as soon as politeness allowed.

Of course she couldn't refuse to return to Bagestan for the wedding, but this time she had come with insurance—Michael's engagement ring on her finger. Now when she was asked whether she intended to make the Return, Jalia could dutifully murmur that she had her future husband to consider. No one could argue with that.

''Why do you say this is a wild-goose chase?''

The Cup Companion's voice broke in on her thoughts. Jalia jolted back into the here and now and gazed at him for a moment.

''You think Noor ran of her own accord, do you?'' she said at last.

''She was seen driving the car herself.''

''And if that's so, it means she's changed her mind about the wedding?''

''Do you doubt it?''

Jalia shrugged. That wasn't her point. ''That being the case, do you honestly imagine that, even assuming we find her, we're just going to bring her meekly back to marry Bari?''

''Women do not always know their own minds,'' Latif said with comfortable masculine arrogance.

It was the kind of thing that made her want to hit him. Jalia sat with her fists clenching in her lap.

"Is that so?"

"Your powers of persuasion may have undermined her. But she will return to her senses when she realizes what she has done. Then she will be glad to know that there is a way back."

"Or perhaps she's come to her senses!" Jalia countered sharply. "That's why she ran. It's a pity it took her so long, that's all."

"But of course—she did not come to her senses until she agreed with you!"

The sarcasm burned like acid.

"She was rushing into marriage with a complete stranger, which would entail a total transformation of her life, and on the basis of what? Nothing more than sex! Would you *encourage* someone to do what Noor was doing?"

He turned and gave her a look of such black emotion she almost quailed. "Why not?" he demanded grimly.

If Noor *had* simply bolted, it was going to cause hideous embarrassment all around, but surely anything was better than to marry in haste? Noor had been totally swept away by Bari's looks and wealth and sex appeal, but that was no foundation for a marriage, still less for uprooting from everything she knew and transplanting to Bagestan.

"For a start, because she's not in love with him! She's blinded by—"

"If she does not love him yet, it will not be long coming. Bari will see to that, once they are married."

Jalia's mouth fell open, angry irritation skittering along her spine. "Oh, a man can make a woman love him, just like that?"

"What kind of man cannot make his own wife love him?"

Her eyes popped with reaction to the arrogance; her mouth opened.

"And how exactly does a man go about it?"

At the look in his eyes now she gasped as if she'd been punched in the stomach.

"Who is your fiancé, that you do not understand a man's power over a woman?" asked the Cup Companion.

Four

Jalia sat up with a jerk. A chasm seemed to be opening up before her, and without having any idea what it represented, she knew it was dangerous.

"What *are* you talking about?" she said mockingly.

The car stopped at a traffic light on the outskirts of Medinat al Bostan. Below them, in the magnificent tapestry that was the city, sunlight gleamed from the golden dome and minarets of the great Shah Jawad mosque and glittered on the sea. It was a heart-stopping sight, she couldn't deny that. Talk about your dreaming spires!

Latif turned and gazed at her for an unnerving few seconds.

"You know what I am talking about," he accused through his teeth.

She didn't, if he meant from personal experience. No man had ever reduced her to adoration on sheer sexual expertise alone, and what he said was just so much masculine arrogance!

"So sex is a crucible in which to melt your wife's independence?"

"Her independence? No. Her dissatisfaction."

"And how many wives are you keeping happy?" she asked sweetly.

"You know that I am not married."

"But when you are, your wife will love you? Oooh, I almost envy her!" she twittered, while a kind of nervous fear zinged up and down her back and she knew that the last woman in the world she'd envy would be Latif Abd al Razzaq's wife. "I *don't* think!"

His eyes burned her.

"So what is the secret of eternal wedded bliss?" Jalia pressed, against the small, wise voice that was advising her to back off.

His jaw tightened at her tone, and he turned with such a look she suddenly found herself breathing through her mouth.

"Do you wish me to show you such secrets in the open road?" he asked, and she was half convinced that if she said yes he would stop the car where it was and reach for her....

"Not me!" she denied hastily, and a smile, or some other emotion, twisted the corner of his mouth. "But if you look around—well, it can't be well-known, or there'd be more happy marriages, wouldn't there? I can't help feeling you could make your fortune marketing this secret."

She was getting under his skin, she could see that, and she pressed her lips together to keep from grinning her triumph at him.

He looked at her again, a narrow, dangerous look, and Jalia's eyes seemed to stretch as she watched him. "In the West, perhaps. But I think even a How To book would not help your fiancé."

"I—what—?" Jalia babbled furiously.

Latif moved his hand from the wheel to where her hand lay on the armrest between them, and with one long, square forefinger fiercely stroked the three opals of her ring.

Jalia snatched her hand away in violent overreaction.

"Do you intend to marry this man?"

"What do you think?"

"I think you would be a fool."

The light changed and he let out the brake and turned his attention to the road. Fury swept over her like a wave. Though he spoke perfect truth, *he* could not know it. She laughed false, angry, deliberately mocking laughter.

"How kind of you to have my interests at heart! But you don't know anything about Michael."

"Yes."

"What, exactly, do you profess to know? You've never even seen him!"

"I have seen you."

"And you don't know anything about me, either!"

"All I need to know for such a judgement."

"And what have you learned about me that allows you to prescribe for my future?" she couldn't stop herself asking, though a moment's thought would have told her she would not come out of the encounter the winner.

He deliberately kept his eyes on the road.

"Your fiancé has never aroused real passion in you," he said grimly.

Jalia jerked back as if he had slapped her. A rage of unfamiliar feeling burned in her abdomen, almost too deep to reach. She felt a primitive, uncharacteristic urge to leap at him, biting and clawing, and teach *him* a lesson in the power of woman.

"How dare you!" she snapped instead, her Western upbringing overruling her wild Eastern blood. She was half aware of her dissatisfaction that it should be so.

His laughter underlined the feebleness of her reply.

"This is what you say to your English boyfriend, I think! Do you expect it to affect such as me?"

"And what would it take to stop *you*? A juggernaut?"

"Ah, if I taught you about love, you would not want me to stop," he declared, a mocking smile lifting one corner of his mouth, and outrage thrilled through her. She knew the last thing on his mind was making love to her. He didn't even like her!

"It'll be a cold day in hell before you teach me about love!" Jalia snapped, as something like panic suddenly choked her. "Suppose we agree that you'll mind your own business when it comes to the intimate details of my love life?"

He was silent. She looked up at his profile and saw that his face was closed, his jaw clamped tight. Disdain was in the very tilt of his jaw as he nodded formally.

''Tell me instead where your cousin will have gone.''

She didn't know how she knew, but she did: the words were a struggle. They were not what he wanted to say.

''I have told you I don't know.''

Although she had demanded it, Jalia was disconcerted by the abrupt change of subject. She had more to say, plenty more, but to go back now and start ranting would look childish.

They were approaching the city centre now: the golden dome appeared only in the gaps between other buildings as they passed.

''You must have some idea.''

''If you're thinking I'm a mind reader, you overestimate me. If you imagine I had prior knowledge, go to hell.''

His eyelids drooped to veil his response to that.

''I am thinking that if your cousin had made friends in al Bostan you would know who they are. Or if she had found a favourite place—a garden or a restaurant—she might have shown it to you.''

My manner is biting off heads. The line of poetry sounded in her head, and he really did look like a roosting hawk now, with his cold green eyes, his beaked nose, his hands on the wheel like talons on a branch. A brilliantly feathered, glittering hawk, owner of his world.

And exerting, for some reason she couldn't fathom, every atom of his self-control.

''She is wearing a white wedding dress and veil, you know. She's not going to be able to just disappear. In a restaurant or any public place she'd attract comment.''

''Where would she go, then?''

Her imagination failed. Where could you hide wearing a staggeringly beautiful pearl-embroidered silk wedding dress with a skirt big enough to cover a football field and a tulle veil five yards long?

Latif put his foot on the brake and drew in to the side of the road, where, under a ragged striped umbrella, a child was selling pomegranates from a battered crate. At the Cup Companion's summons the boy jumped up to thrust a half dozen pomegranates into a much-used plastic bag, and carried it to the car.

As Latif passed over the money he asked a question, which Jalia could just about follow. The urchin's response she couldn't understand at all, but from his excited hand signals she guessed that he had seen Noor pass.

Latif set the bag of fruit into the back seat beside his sword and put the car in motion.

''What did he say?''

''He saw a big white car go past with a woman at the wheel and a white flag streaming from the roof,'' he reported with a smile twitching at the corner of his mouth. ''About half an hour ago. Another man in a car asked him the same question soon after. The white car hasn't come back. He's not sure about the other.''

''A white flag!'' Jalia exclaimed. ''Why would she be flying a white flag?''

''To signal her surrender?''

His dry voice made her want to laugh, but she suppressed the desire. She had no intention of getting pally with the man.

They were in the city centre now. Latif began cruising the streets, turning here and there at random. As best she could, Jalia monitored passing cars as well as those parked at the side of the road. She glanced down each side street as they passed.

Jalia sighed.

"Oh, if this isn't just Noor all over!" she muttered. "Turn a deaf ear to everything until it suits her! If she'd listened to me when I was talking to her—if she'd actually sat down and considered what I was saying, she would have come to this conclusion long ago. Instead she waits until it's almost too late and will cause the maximum chaos!"

Latif threw her a look. "Or you might say that if you hadn't tried to force your views on her so unnecessarily, there would have been no fear suddenly erupting in her and taking over."

"You say unnecessarily, I say necessarily…" Jalia sang in bright mockery, then glowered at him. "Why are you right and I'm wrong?"

"I?" he demanded sharply. "It is Bari and Noor's judgement that you challenged, not mine! I have no opinion, except that when two people decide to get married they should be left to make their own fate!"

She whooped with outrage.

"And what were you saying to me not twenty minutes ago?" she shrieked. "Were you advising me not to marry Michael, or was I hallucinating? *You would be a fool to marry this man!*" she cited sharply. "Was that what you said, or do I misquote you?"

His eyes met hers, and she sensed a kind of shock in his gaze. A muscle in his cheek twitched, but whether with annoyance or an impulse to laugh she couldn't tell. It *was* funny, but she was too annoyed to find it so.

"You blame your cousin for not giving serious consideration to your doubts about her engagement, but you do not listen to my doubts about yours. Who has the double standard now?" he said, with the air of a man pulling a brand from the burning.

Laughter trembled in her throat, but she was afraid of letting her guard down with him. Jalia bit her lip.

"Great! We're both hypocrites," she said, shaking her head.

Instead of making a reply to that, Latif jerked forward to stare out the window.

"*Barakullah!*" he breathed.

He had turned into the wide boulevard that led down to the seafront. At the bottom was the broad, sparkling expanse of the Gulf of Barakat, and miles of bright sky.

Jalia narrowed her eyes against the glitter. Off to the right a forest of silver masts marked the yacht basin.

"A yacht!" she cried. "Of course! I'll bet she knows someone on a boat—maybe some friend even sailed over for the wedding. The perfect hide—"

"Look up," Latif interrupted. He stretched an arm past her head, pointing into the sky, where a little plane glinted in the sun as it headed up the coast towards the mountains.

"That plane? What, do you think—?"

"It is Bari's plane."

Jalia gasped hoarsely. "Are you sure?"

"We can confirm it soon enough."

"But what—?" Jalia fell silent; there was no point

babbling questions to which neither of them had answers.

Latif turned the car along the shore highway. After a few minutes he turned in under an arched gateway in a high wall, and she saw a small brick-and-glass building and a sign announcing the Island Air Taxi service to the Gulf Eden Resort.

Out on the water several small planes were moored, bouncing gently in the swell. Latif stepped on the brakes and pointed again. Ahead of them on the tarmac, carelessly taking up three parking spaces, as if the driver had been in too much of a hurry to care, sat a large white limousine, parked and empty.

They slipped out of the car.

"Is that it? Is that the al Khalids' limousine?" she asked.

He nodded thoughtfully.

"My God," Jalia breathed. She felt completely stunned. She stared up at the glinting silver bird in the distance. "Is Noor at the controls, do you think? Why? Where can she be going? And where's Bari?"

Latif turned his head to run his eyes over the half dozen other cars in the lot, then shook his head.

"His car is not here."

She stared up at the plane as if the sight of it would tell her something. A gust of wind struck her, blowing the green silk tunic wildly against her body. She felt a blast of fine sand against her cheek.

Latif stiffened to attention beside her. He was still looking into the sky, but not at the plane. Frowning, Jalia turned her head to follow his gaze.

In the past few minutes a mass of cloud had boiled up from behind the mountains, and even as she watched it was growing, rushing to shroud the sky over the city.

Over the water the sky was still a clear, hot blue, but that couldn't last. Jalia turned her head again to stare at the plane, watching anxiously for some sign that it was banking, turning, that the pilot had seen the clouds building and made the decision to put down again.

But the little plane, the sun glinting from its fat wings, sailed serenely on.

Five

There was little sleep for anyone in the palace that night. The phones rang constantly, with family and friends in the country and abroad calling for news, calls from officials organizing the search team, and journalists around the world clogging up the line asking for details of Princess Noor's Fatal Peril.

Everybody felt worse when the couple's disappearance began to be announced on repeated television news bulletins in the early evening and the announcer's voice resonated with the kind of gravity that meant he thought Princess Noor was probably dead.

But they couldn't just turn it off. It was entirely possible that some reporter would get wind of a search team discovery and broadcast the news before the family was notified. The regular announcements became a horrible kind of compulsive listening for them all as more and more journalists joined the fray.

On the breakfast terrace early the next morning, bleary-eyed but unable to sleep, and fed up with the constant insensitive badgering, Jalia delivered herself of a few blistering comments to one journalist and hung up the phone to find Latif watching her.

He was silhouetted against the morning sun, and she couldn't see his expression. She dropped her eyes and picked up her coffee.

"Is there any news?" she asked. The question had taken on the impact of ritual. They were all constantly asking it of each other.

"Have you heard that the Barakat Emirates have sent a couple of planes to join the search this morning?"

Jalia nodded.

Latif set something on the ground, then moved over to pour himself a cup of coffee. "Then there's no news."

"God, how I hate sitting here doing nothing more productive than fielding calls from the media. If only there was something to *do!*" she exploded. Part of the emptiness she felt was the letdown after the blizzard of wedding preparations, of course. But Jalia was also missing the hard, rewarding work of her university life.

Latif remained standing, resting his hips back against the table, gazing out over the courtyard. He swirled the coffee in his cup.

"Well, why not?"

Jalia looked up, and his eyes turned to her with a hooded expression she couldn't fathom. "What do you mean, why not?'' Suddenly her eye fell on the case he had set down by a column. She frowned in sudden dismay.

"Are you leaving?" How could he go when they were in such trouble? Bari was one of his closest friends!

He took another sip of coffee. "I'm going to drive up into the mountains to ask in the villages whether anyone saw or heard a plane coming down in the storm."

She stared at him, the fog of a sleepless night abruptly clearing from her brain. "What a brilliant idea!" she breathed. "I wish I could do something useful like that!"

Latif shrugged as if she impressed him not at all. "Why don't you?"

"It would take me a week to decipher the answers." The mountain dialects of both Bagestani Arabic and Parvani, Bagestan's two languages, were very different from what was spoken in the cities, and Jalia had trouble enough even in the city.

Latif said nothing, merely turned, set down his cup, and rang the bell. A servant came out and asked what he would eat. Latif shook his head.

"I don't want food, thanks, Mansour," he began in Arabic. "You have a son named Shafi."

"God be thanked. Fifteen years old, a strong healthy boy. A very good son."

"I am going into the mountains to help the search," Latif explained. "I will need another pair of eyes. Would you allow Shafi to accompany and assist me? I may be gone several days."

Mansour's expression was pained as he clasped his

fist to his chest. "Willingly, Lord! But alas, he is not at home! As you know, he—"

"Thank you, Mansour," Latif interrupted him.

The servant turned to go, but Jalia called him back.

"I beg that thou be so good as to bring His Excellency some food wherewith to break his fast, if it please thee," she said in her formal, antiquated Arabic. And to Latif, "You ought to eat something if you're going on the road."

Latif laughed aloud and turned to the servant. "An omelette, then, Mansour."

Mansour bowed and went back inside. In the tree a bird sang entrancingly, but could not lighten the gloom and worry in Jalia's heart.

"What are you going to do?" Jalia asked.

Latif pulled out a chair. "I have no specific plan," he said, sitting down opposite her. He reached for the warmed bread left on her plate with a kind of intimate assumption of her permission, and tore a bite-sized piece off with long, strong fingers. "The mountain villages don't get television and they don't have phones. So the only way to—"

"I meant, who will you take with you to be the extra pair of eyes?"

He shrugged. "It's not important."

But of course it was. How could his search be effective if he had to watch the road the whole time?

"I'm not doing anything. I should have been going home tomorrow, but I can't leave with Noor missing," she offered hesitantly. "I could go with you, if you liked."

Latif's mouth tightened. "I expect to search until

something definite turns up," he said stiffly. "I may be away several days."

"Where will you sleep at night?"

"Sometimes in village rest houses, sometimes under the stars. Whatever comes. It won't be comfortable. And there may be fleas in the rest houses."

Maybe it was his obvious reluctance that hardened the momentary impulse into determination. This was her chance to get away from the media, the phone and the helpless speculation and do something actively useful.

"Better fleas with a chance to help," she said, who had never had a fleabite in her life, "than sitting with my mother and aunt, worrying uselessly."

She could see that Latif didn't like the idea, and of course she didn't relish being with him, but what would that matter if they found Noor and Bari?

"Don't you think you'll do better with another pair of eyes?" she pressed.

His eyes rested on her face with an unreadable expression.

"She's my cousin, Latif."

"And he's my friend. But conditions will be primitive."

"What gave you the idea I expect to be pampered?"

"There's a lot of ground between primitive and pampered, Princess."

A glint in his eyes made her think he was deliberately baiting her as a way of resisting her suggestion, but his resistance only fuelled her determination. She stifled her irritation, always so quick to ignite in his presence.

"You won't be able to look around for signs of the plane as you drive if you go alone. You'll need your concentration for the road—especially those twisty, rugged mountain roads," she argued. "And even supposing you did find them, how would you cope with…"

She trailed off. In a sudden moment of clarity, as if she had come out of a trance, or lifted her head out of water, the thought appeared in her head: *Travel around the countryside with only Latif Abd al Razzaq for company? Are you crazy?*

What demon had possessed her?

"Oh, never m—" she began. But she had come to her senses too late.

"No, you are right. Two will be much more effective than one. Thank you, I will be glad of your help. Pack something warm. It gets cold in the mountains at night," said Latif Abd al Razzaq as the trap closed on her. "We will leave in an hour."

"Do you have a plan in mind?" Jalia asked as the road began to climb and the mountains rose over them, dangerous and seductive, like Latif himself.

Jalia was lying in the bed she had made, though she had done her best to unmake it. She had rushed to tell her mother about the trip, hoping for a reprise of the old *this is not the West, this is Bagestan, and we must not offend people by violating their customs* argument. But when she had gently hinted that people might be shocked if she drove around with a man not related to her, her mother had only shrugged.

"Ghasib ran a secular government for over thirty years, and people here have more casual attitudes now. If you meet someone disapproving, just say Latif is your husband.''

''Thanks, Mother!'' Jalia snapped. ''And then they'll put us in the same bed! I don't think so!''

Her mother lifted her hands. ''Then say he is your bodyguard. For goodness' sake, Jalia, who would have guessed you would be so old-fashioned? Noor is missing. Your aunt is out of her mind with worry! If you have to put up with the company of a man you don't like for a few days to help find your cousin, surely that's a small price to pay?''

Which was quite true. Noor's parents had been hugely kind to Jalia all her life, giving her fabulous holidays in Australia every year since she was a child. They had always treated her very kindly on those long childhood visits.

Of course she was grateful to them. Noor was like a sister to her—spoiled and exasperating, but nevertheless loving and loved.

And yet, it was with a feeling of somehow having been outmanoeuvred that Jalia had joined Latif and tossed her pack into the four-wheel drive.

''Plan?'' Latif responded now. ''My plan is to follow the advice of Mulla Nasruddin.''

The name was familiar: it signified a joke figure in folktales, but Jalia hadn't paid much attention to the ancient stories since she was a teenager.

She frowned a question, and Latif explained,

''One day one of his neighbours discovered the Mulla on his hands and knees under a street lamp near his house and stopped to ask what the problem was.

'''I am looking for my house key, which I have dropped,' said the Mulla.

"The helpful neighbour immediately dropped to his knees and joined the Mulla in the search. After some time, the key had not turned up.

"'Where exactly were you when you dropped your key?' the neighbour asked at last.

"'Standing at my front door,' said Mulla.

"The neighbour stared. 'But in that case why are you searching here in the street, yards from your house?'

"Mulla Nasruddin drew himself up. 'Have you not noticed,' he said, 'that *this* is where the *light* is?'"

One corner of Latif's mouth curved up as he finished the tale, and Jalia laughed. He told the story well.

"But I'm not sure I get the point," she confessed.

Latif flicked her a smile. "We don't know where the plane went down. But we will look for it where we *can* look."

Jalia laughed softly; they exchanged a look; and suddenly a powerful connection was flowing between them that was very different from the suppressed hostility she usually felt.

A jolt of awareness socked through her. For the first time she realized how deeply attractive a man Latif was—not just physically, with his black hair, his falcon's looks and his smoothly muscled body, but mentally.

But what did that matter? She wasn't attracted to him, and even if she were, nothing would induce her to turn her back on the life she had created for herself and come to Bagestan.

She knew without asking that Latif Abd al Razzaq was inextricably bound to Bagestan. He had worked and struggled for years to assist the Sultan to the throne.

So there was no need for her heart to start beating as if she had discovered danger.

The woman moved smilingly around her simple house, dressed in one of the most gorgeous outfits Jalia had ever seen anyone make mint tea in—a wine-red velvet skirt and long tunic trimmed around neck, hem and cuffs with gold braid and shimmering gold medallions, almost as elaborately beautiful as the bridesmaids' outfits at Noor's wedding.

Over her waist-length black hair a gauzy black scarf glinted with more medallions. Her arms were circled with dozens of bracelets; black, kohl-rimmed eyes breathed the power and mystery of the feminine.

The mountain tribeswomen were known for the luxury of their daily dress, and Jalia couldn't help wondering what effect it would have on the psyche to get up every morning and dress in such finery. In front of the house a young girl, similarly dressed, expertly kept her veil in check as she pounded spice in a stone mortar. The sharp, pungent odour filled the air.

"It is well that the Sultan has come back," the woman was saying, and either this village dialect was extremely pure, or her own ear was acclimatizing after a few days, because Jalia could understand her with little problem. "Please tell him that whenever he wishes to call he, too, will be an honoured guest in our house."

She was laying out a huge meal for them, on the traditional cloth spread on the ground under a tree.

Jalia was horrified by the amount of food being prepared for them, for these were obviously poor people. The woman's husband, she had told them, gathered firewood and sold it in the village to eke out the living from their farm.

"But what will they eat tomorrow if we eat all their food today?" she demanded of Latif when the woman left them alone.

He lifted his eyebrows at her. "God will provide."

"After three years of drought," she pointed out dryly.

"You are too Western," Latif said. "Do you think we have adopted Western generosity here—to give only what does not cost us? Here in the mountains, generosity is generosity. Do you not know the story of Anwar Beg?"

She sometimes felt with him that she was in a book.

"Tell me."

"He had a magnificent horse, which a friend of his wished to buy. But however high the price, however hard he negotiated, Anwar Beg would not part with his prize beast, and at last the man was forced to give up.

"Then one day he heard that Anwar Beg had fallen on hard times, and hardly had food to put on the table. He said to himself, now he will have to sell that wonderful horse of his, and he went to Anwar Beg's house.

"Anwar Beg invited him in, and his friend sat down and tried to open negotiations. But Anwar Beg stopped him. 'You are my guest. First there is the matter of hospitality,' he insisted.

"So the two men waited while the meal Anwar Beg ordered to be prepared for him was cooked and served. Scarcely containing his impatience, his friend ate the delicious meat stew that was brought, complimenting his host on the meal.

"'Friend,' said the man when the meal was finished, 'I wish to make you an offer again on that magnificent horse which you have always refused to sell.'

"Anwar Beg shook his head. 'Impossible,' he said.

"'But surely, with things with you as they now are,'' the neighbour cried, 'you must listen to reason! Sell me the horse! I will give you a good price for it so that you can provide for your family.'

"'It is impossible,' repeated Anwar Beg. 'You came to me as a guest, and it was necessary to show you hospitality. Having no other food to offer you, I ordered that the horse be slaughtered to make the stew you have just eaten.'"

Jalia gazed at Latif a long time when the story was finished, and predominant among her feelings was guilt. "I could never live up to a standard like that," she said quietly.

"Yes," he contradicted her. "This story describes not what is, but what we strive towards. You have a more generous spirit than you know—it is in your eyes. And in your blood. The al Jawadi have a tradition of great generosity.

"Think of your grandfather's generous treatment of the young orphan boy, Ghasib, who grew up to betray him. This is the blood you have inherited, Jalia, whether you know it or not. And when you stop being afraid, then you will find your generosity."

He was always saying things like that, what she called his "gnomic utterances."

"When I stop being afraid of what?" she asked, indignant.

"I cannot do all the work for you. Some things you must discover for yourself," he said, and in his voice was an urgency that frightened her.

Six

Latif kept his eyes on the road. It was all he could do not to shout at her, so angry was he—at her wilful blindness, at fate, at himself.

Himself. Why should he blame her, or fate, when his trouble was of his own making? Fate had put her in his way; he had doubted fate's wisdom, as fools do. He had been too cautious in embracing the way fate showed him, and now he could never embrace her as his wife....

"Princess Muna, Sheikh Ihsan," Ashraf had said, "here is my trusted Cup Companion, my ally and support throughout our struggle. Latif Abd al Razzaq Shahin will aid you and your family...."

The rest of what the new Sultan said was lost in the clamour in Latif's head. For, standing beside Princess Muna and her husband, watching him with a clear, level gaze, was the woman he had been waiting for since that moment his soul had been plucked from its nest beside her in the heavens and sent into the cruel, testing world.

A stern nobility, which must have told anyone who looked at her that she was of royal blood, was evident in the set of her mouth, the lift of her head.

In addition she had an unusual, harsh beauty, proud and unapproachable. Her eyes were coolly intelligent as she gazed at him, and he felt that only he could see through to the secret of a passionately generous heart.

All that he saw between one painful heartbeat and another.

The thick fair hair had seemed like a fall of honey against her cheek, the promise of sweetness so tangible he had to clench his fists not to wrap his hand in its silky strands, bend closer to inhale the odour, bury his mouth in the taste.

''...Jalia...'' he heard through the drumming of his heart, and with a fist at his breast, he bowed.

''Princess Jalia,'' he said. His voice must have told her what he felt, how he took her name into himself, took her, possessed her self and her name forever by speaking two words that changed his life....

''I don't use that title,'' she had responded with chilly disdain, cutting through the haze that enveloped his brain with the frosted blade of hauteur. ''My name is Jalia Shahbazi, Your Excellency.''

Like a man on a journey faced with an ice-topped mountain in his path, he had advised caution to his heart. She was hostile and guarded, and he couldn't guess why.

Logic told him that nothing would be gained by a direct assault. He must give her time.

Weak, cowardly thought that it was, his heart had given it room, had considered it, had bowed to the dictates of logic when deep instinct told him that he must challenge her, that his own passion's fire would melt the ice in which her heart was encased.

He had given her time, but time was not his to give. Within days she had fled back to the cold northern country of her birth.

She had given no warning of her departure. Merely the next time he had met her parents and asked for her, he learned that she had gone "home" that morning.

For the next few weeks, carrying out his duties for the Sultan, advising Jalia's parents about their lost properties and treasures, helping them in their plans to return to Bagestan, he had called himself a fool. To be so blinded by a woman's beauty, to be so challenged by a cold demeanour—it was no more than a fool's obsession, a child seeing what it can't have and wanting it because of that.

Angry with her for her coldness, angry with himself for his heat, telling himself his heart was not truly engaged—so he had passed the time until the day of her cousin's wedding to his friend had approached, and Jalia had reluctantly returned to Bagestan.

And now she was wearing a ring. Another man's ring.

The first time he had seen her he had been deafened by the thunder and rushing of his own blood. This time he had been blinded—by a haze of anguished fury that ripped at him. Broken heart? he remembered thinking dimly. Whoever felt so weak a torment had never known love: Latif's heart had been set upon by wild dogs and torn to pieces. He would never put it together again.

It waved at her from the top of a ridge, a soft silver hand catching the sunlight with a syncopated rhythm of glimmer under the bright sun, a liquid mirror. The breath hissed between her teeth as she groped for the binoculars against her chest.

"Something?"

The truck slowed, and she nodded once as she fitted the glasses to her eyes. "Something large and metallic. Moving in the wind."

Latif Abd al Razzaq pulled the four-wheel drive off the road and stopped, and Jalia combed the ridge with the binoculars to find it again.

"There," she said. It was a chunk of aluminum, perhaps, silver but not necessarily with the glitter of newly ripped-apart metal, not necessarily part of a plane that has crashed taking two young and vital human beings to a wasteful death.

"I can't tell what it is."

But he had already turned off the engine and now stepped out on the grey-and-brown mountainside. Jalia scrambled to follow.

A familiar sense of dread dragged at her. In the past few days there had been a half dozen times when she had seen something that might have marked wreckage from a downed plane, and each time her heart beat a frantic, anxious message in her temples, weighted down her stomach so that she felt old.

She clambered after him across the rugged, half

breathtaking, half terrifying landscape, towards the ridge of rock overlooking a crevasse. Behind it the mountainside rose sheer and raw, making her dizzy.

If the plane had crashed here and gone over the edge...how far down was the floor of the crevasse behind that ridge?

The last few yards were difficult, and she was panting with fear and exertion as she approached the edge. Above her, Latif reached the object she had seen and knelt down to examine it.

"A cargo door," he said as she came up, and her hand flew to her mouth.

"Oh, God!" It lay broken and torn where it had been caught on a sharp rock and prevented from falling over the edge. A thin strip of torn shiny metal attached to a hinge waved in the air. "Was there—is it part of Bari's plane?"

A sudden breeze caught the glittering aluminum, and her heart fluttered in time with it. Jalia dropped flat on her stomach and peered over the rocky ridge.

"No, it is too big. Part of a commercial or military aircraft, lost in flight. It has been here for a long time," Latif said.

"Oh, thank God! Are you sure?" Her constricted lungs opened again, her heart calmed. She believed him, but still she put the binoculars to her eyes and peered over the ridge to get a view of the bottom.

She wasn't sure what hope there could be, if the plane had come down anywhere in the mountains. But she hated to imagine it pitching down into terrain like this.

"There's a *valley!*" she cried. Nestling down among the crags was a wide green oval, thriving with life. She took the glasses from her eyes and peered down, half disbelieving.

"From the road you'd never guess it was there!" At either end of the valley two thrusting formations of rock created a kind of optical illusion when she looked up, seeming much closer together than they were.

"Look at those two peaks at either end! From this angle, don't they look like falcons or hawks or something? What a beautiful place."

"Royal falcons," he said. "They are called the *Shahins*."

She became aware of a sense of peace surrounding her. In the far distance Mount Shir presided over all, a brooding presence, dangerous and protective at the same time, the powerful mother-father of the lands that pressed against her like suckling infants.

Jalia lifted her head and gazed up at the rich blue sky. Suddenly she understood that her defensive attitude towards this country had prevented her truly seeing it.

Now, for once, she allowed herself to see what she was looking at, to feel the air that surrounded her. It was so fresh, so pure. And it seemed charged with energy, as if the great mountain were a generator.

"This really is a wonderful place," she murmured and, turning to share it with Latif, she smiled at him. "I'm beginning to understand why my mother and father never lost their hope of returning home."

She gazed down at the valley again. There weren't words to describe the calm and beauty that lay over the scene.

"I can see goats! And farms—how can it be so

green after such a long drought, I wonder? So many trees. Do you know the name of the valley?'' she demanded, thinking she would not be surprised to hear him say *Shangri-La.*

"We call it Sey-Shahin,'' he said. "Three Falcons.''

She turned to look into his face, her eyebrows climbing with surprised enquiry.

"Yes, this is my home,'' said Latif Abd al Razzaq Shahin. "Outsiders give us, and the valley, the name Marzuqi.''

"Marzuqi,'' Jalia repeated softly. *The Blessed.* She could see how the valley had achieved the name. It looked fertile and protected, and as old as time.

"It's so green,'' she said, feeling how inadequate the word was to describe what she saw and felt.

"The drought did not affect us so badly here, so when the rains came, the fields recovered quickly.''

Jalia glanced around. "Can we go down? Where is the road?''

The valley looked at first glance to be completely surrounded by impenetrable, unyielding rock. But Latif pointed across the valley to where a grey line emerged from a dark circle like an egg under the feet of the falcon-shaped rock, and slanted slowly down to the valley floor.

"That is the tunnel. The road has been badly damaged by the heavy rains since the drought ended. At the moment the way in and out is on foot, or by mule.''

"My God, how will people manage?''

A pebble was dislodged under her elbow and went over the edge to bounce down and down. She watched it with a curious feeling that the movement had significance.

"We are used to it. The road is only a few years old, and was badly made. Ghasib finally forced the tunnel through because every time he sent his administrators to the valley they lost their way in the passes. Some say that Genghis Khan had the same difficulty."

Jalia laughed and clapped her hands together in delight. "So this is the valley that was never conquered?"

"Even Islam came to Sey-Shahin very late. There are many ancient rituals among our people that exist nowhere else in the world. Western scholars sometimes wish to come here to study what they call 'living tradition'—hoping to find a mirror of the past in the present practices of the Marzuqi people."

She frowned in thought. "I remember someone in the department coming on a field trip here a few years ago with very high hopes. But I don't think—"

She stopped because of his expression. "What happened? Do you know?"

"Possibly he got lost in the passes," Latif said guilelessly, and Jalia erupted in a burst of laughter, then clapped her hands over her mouth and sat gazing up at him, her eyes alight.

His eyes met hers in shared amusement, and she felt a treacherous prickle along her spine that said it was not only the land her prejudices had prevented her seeing clearly.

"The only experienced guides in this area are Sey-Shahini tribesmen. Sometimes a bribe is high enough, and someone slips through. That encourages others to think that such bribes work. Guides used to make a living in summer from failing to find the valley.''

She was laughing, though God alone knew why. Being an academic herself, she ought to have regretted the thwarting of scholarship.

But the valley looked so enchanting that something in her did not want to think of its people being analysed and ''published.''

Her blood was stronger than her academic loyalties, maybe. Certainly as she gazed down at the flourishing little valley, her heart was drawn there.

''Suppose *I* wanted to—''

The expression on Latif's face struck her a blow that left her breathless, and choked the words in her throat. He was looking at her as if that was exactly the question he wanted to hear.

A chasm opened in front of her, without warning, dangerous and deep, as Jalia understood that she had been mistaken in his feelings all this time. Latif Abd al Razzaq might be angry, he might be impatient, but it wasn't dislike that was motivating him.

He wanted her. It was there in the fierce emerald eyes, in the set of his jaw, in the way his hand gripped the rock he leaned against—as if he held it to prevent himself from reaching for her. Every muscle and ligament now shouted the truth that she should have heard weeks ago—had heard, perhaps, and had run from.

But blindly. Like a terrified fool in the dark she had run straight into danger, straight into the falcon's nest.

Suddenly she saw it—the whole process by which he had brought her here, out into the starkly beautiful land of her ancestors, to the heart of his own existence, to a state of mind where she could no longer deny the land's deep and abiding hold over her heart and blood. It was a trap, baited with the simplest psychological techniques.

This was what her parents had hoped for—that the country would somehow get to her. That the land and the people would convince her where words could not.

What a fool she had been, playing with so potent a danger as a man like Latif Abd al Razzaq. Her first instinct had been right—to run. She should never have come back to Bagestan, ring or no ring. What good would a ring do if her own heart betrayed her?

The silence extended while he watched the play of emotion on her stern, beautiful face.

"What did you want to say?"

"Nothing," said Jalia. "We'd better get going."

She was under threat. She knew it. Back in the little truck she watched Latif's profile surreptitiously, and reminded herself that she didn't go for the dark, eagle-eyed look.

And yet…oh, how his masculinity emanated from him, reaching out and touching her with an aura that said, *I am a man. You are a woman.*

She might not go for his type, but from the beginning she had instinctively felt that there was something about Latif that spelled danger for her. She should have done anything rather than let herself get into this vehicle with him and head off into a country of stark beauty with no time limit and no destination.

But she knew it too late.

They got lost in the passes. Jalia looked around her as they drove over the rough stony road. My God, and well they might! she thought. The road itself was sometimes hardly discernible to an untrained eye; could she be sure of following it even five miles?

If she tried to get away from Latif up here she'd be the Woman Who Never Returned. They'd find her skeleton in twenty-five years...

She was stuck with him. Because she knew without asking that he would not turn around and take her back home. And she was afraid to ask, for fear of what the asking would tell him.

She was watching him, hardly aware of her own focus, in a state near panic. He was so attractive, so vital, like a healthy wild animal. His blood seemed to pulse with life just under his skin.

And he was getting under hers. He always had, if only she'd had the wit to realize it. *This* was why she'd run home after the Coronation. It was why she was wearing Michael's engagement ring right now.

Not because of some nameless threat from her parents, but because she was on a precipice with Latif Abd al Razzaq, as surely as the pebble she had knocked over the ridge to the valley.

Seven

Night closed in quickly in the mountains. As darkness fell Jalia sat by their campfire on a plateau, watching the sunset.

In the broad rugged pass they were travelling through, the villages were few and far between. Below, a boy followed a couple of skinny goats along a sloping path, his lazy switch urging them home. In the little village on the edge of the valley, a white cloth hung on a line, flapping in the breeze. Smoke trickled up from a hearth fire.

She wondered who was tending that fire, and whether that woman's life was anything like her own.

It was Sey-Shahin Valley again, but from a different vantage point, for the road had twisted away from the valley for the past few days as it fought its way through the passes.

Last night they had stayed in a small village clinging to a rugged slope. It was the last village they had
seen.

Today they had travelled a whole day through
bleak, empty passes, in a large erratic circle around
the base of one giant falcon-shaped peak.

The road had finally led down into the tunnel hewn
through the living rock. An hour ago they had
emerged onto a narrow plateau, with the valley spread
out below them.

To one side, a tiny waterfall showed where a mountain stream tentatively flowed again after the years of
drought. There they had found a level, lightly wooded
spot to pitch their tent.

The haunting sound of goats' bells and a distant
muezzin mingled on the clear air. The sun was going
down in flames behind the mountains, and in the long,
lonely shadows all around her lay a starkly beautiful
landscape dominated by the two rocky sentinels, one
towering above her, one on the opposite side of the
green valley.

Over all brooded the ever-present, distant white
peak now bathed in liquid gold, Mount Shir.

Jalia wished it were not so beautiful. Out here,
face-to-face with the land, she found that it pulled at
her heart with a feeling that was almost pain. From
the beginning of the adventure this yearning for the
might-have-been had been aching in her, just beyond
the reach of consciousness.

Since her first view of Sey-Shahin Valley, though,
she had been sharply aware of it: if Ghasib had never
betrayed her grandfather, this would have been her
country. She would have been familiar with these

crags and passes, with the magical green valleys, with
the handsome and courageous people who lived here,
where life held such different values than those she
had grown up among.

And where she might have thrilled with delight
when Latif Abd al Razzaq took command of every
situation and of her, looked at her with possessive
eyes, told her what a man could do to make his wife
love him....

The memory of that conversation in the car on the
day of Noor's disappearance had been called up again
since her moment of enlightenment overlooking his
valley home, and now, with the birds in the valley
singing the sun down, the air crisp and clear all
around, and water set for boiling in the fire she
tended, it summoned up in her a fierce longing.

What Latif had spoken of was part of the mountain
warrior's code in the land that should have been the
land of her birth—bravery in battle, generosity to
friends, hospitality to strangers, and for your
wife...virile lovemaking.

At the time, sitting in the car beside him, feeling
so attacked by his disapproval, she had been sure Latif had said what he had merely to be provocative.
But after that strange silent exchange on the crag
overlooking the valley, something had changed between them.

Now her imagination kept revisiting earlier moments, reassessing what she had seen and felt from
him. And now, when it was too late to do her any
good, the truth of that conversation in the car seemed
so wildly obvious she could hardly believe she'd
missed it—Latif had spoken the way he did because

he was attracted to her. Because, in spite of his denial, he *had* imagined teaching her—what had he said?— *a man's power over a woman.* Even then.

And the attraction had not lessened with proximity. What a fool she had been to come with him on this fruitless search! Instead of saving Noor, she had put herself in danger.

She could feel the intensity of his desire, as if the air thickened around them, whenever he approached, and it was getting more powerful and impossible to ignore by the hour.

She could feel it now, when he was out there in the shadows somewhere, hunting. It was over her like a cloak, a blanket of sexual heat, stroking her hair, kissing her skin with a hunger unlike anything she had dreamed possible.

How had she not understood it from the beginning? How had she been so blind?

Need burned like honey in her muscles as she remembered his eyes, his deep voice, making her stretch slowly and lift the heavy fall of hair from the back of her neck while an unfamiliar sensuousness warmed her, and she heard his voice again in her head.

Who is your fiancé, that you do not understand a man's power over a woman?

She raised her head, and Latif was there, standing in the black shadows on the other side of the fire, watching her with a face like a brigand's, the face of a man who sees what he wants and means to take it.

Jalia's eyes widened as she stared up at him, double flames leaping in her half entranced, half frightened gaze, her hands frozen in her own hair, sensual need making all her movements languid with unconscious erotic temptation.

He could take her now—the truth was there in her eyes. For one night he could make her his.

This night.

Latif's gaze licked around her with flame hotter than the fire. His lips parted for a moment, then closed resolutely. She saw how passionately full his mouth was, and how iron control held it firm. If a man like him ever let go...

If the mountain beneath her cracked from side to side...

Without a word he turned away and bent to drive a notched stake at one side of the fire with neat blows from his axe. Then a second, on the other side. He set a third, thinner stick to rest on the notches. On it was a small animal carcass, neatly skinned. The flesh began to hiss and blacken as the fire licked it.

Later they lay side by side in their sleeping bags with the night all around them. Overhead the stars gleamed against the lush black fabric of the sky, dense and rich, and so far away.

She was bone tired, she was well fed, but still she couldn't sleep. Jalia lay gazing up at the stars, wondering which of the thousands of sparkles she saw were still alive, and which had died before the earth gave birth to life, yet still sent their light through the void to thrill her.

She felt Latif stir beside her, and turned her gaze. He was lying on his back, his hands crossed under his head. She saw starlight reflected in his eyes. He couldn't sleep either, and she knew why.

It would be dangerous, oh so dangerous, to let him love her. And yet, for one night, just one night...

"Tell me a story," she begged softly.

He turned his head towards her, so that the light was lost from his eyes and she only sensed the way his gaze touched her, dark and probing, almost angry.

"A story?"

"You always have some story that's relevant to whatever situation we're in. Haven't you got a relevant story now?"

"Relevant to what part of this situation, Jalia?" his voice asked softly, and she suddenly felt that where softness was, there lurked danger. "To our search for your runaway cousin, who may have died for a foolish fear? Or to our desire for each other, which we pretend not to be consumed by even though it burns us like a drought every minute, every second we are alive?"

Jalia gasped. Need flamed over her, burning and desperate, because he had put it into words.

"Latif—" she protested. Whether she would have begged him to love her, or to leave her alone, she really didn't know. But whatever she might have said was lost when he spoke.

"A story, you say. Shall I tell you the story of how my desire grew, Jalia? But it did not grow. It was born a giant. In the first moment that I looked at you it was already too big, too powerful, too overwhelming to kill.

"I could only trap it, like a tiger in a net of ropes, hampered, bedevilled, unable to run, made mad by its confinement. Is this the story I should tell you? And what will you tell me in return?"

He paused, and she licked her lips, but no word came.

"You came to this country determined to hate it, to resist it, to reject its claim on you and your mind and heart. I saw this and still I could not stop my heart's knowing that you are mine. You belong to me, Jalia—my heart, my mind, my body, my soul…all that I am says that it is so."

She was shivering with reaction, with fear and dismay. This was more, so much more than she had imagined. This, then, was what she had protected herself against when she put Michael's ring on her finger.

"No," she said, her heart fluttering with panic.

"No," he agreed harshly. "I know it. You have said it every way you can. After the Coronation, before I could try to tell you, to make you see, you fled me. Didn't you? You ran from me because you knew without my telling you.

"I would have hidden it, I would have played the slow game, the Western game, where a man pretends he does not want a woman—or maybe it is not a pretence. How does a man see what his whole life depends on and then pretend he does not need it?

"You knew how it was with me. But I did not know you knew until you had run away from me.

"I could not chase after you, to that cold country where you live, not when there was so much for me here, so much work that every day, every hour counts. And even if I had gone to bring you back—you are a woman who does not love this country. Was it right that I should go after you, bring you home, make you mine, when your whole heart could not be here?

"I said to myself, I will let her go. A man does not love forever in one moment."

Chills coursed over and through her, of an emotion so powerful it was like drowning.

"That was my foolishness, to think so," he went on, his deep voice beating with emotion like a drum. "You are mine, and it has been so since the first moment. Nothing changes that, whether you stay or go, whether you admit it or not.

"You are mine because my heart bound itself to yours before you were born. Because fate made us one heart and then divided it, and now I have found you again."

She tasted salt on her lips, and discovered that she was crying. Tears of grief because of who she was, because she couldn't be the woman she might once have been, that woman whose heart could go to him freely, who could see her fate, her whole life, in a man's words.

"Oh, Latif," she whispered desperately.

"No," he said, "I must tell you the story you asked for. Here in the land that is mine, I must tell you. You came back, but not to me. You were next to me, but out of reach. You came back with a ring that tells me you belong to another man. That is our story, Jalia."

Eight

He raised himself on one elbow beside her, and his head blotted out the rising moon. It was a welcome darkness, a darkness in which anything was possible, and without conscious thought, driven by a hunger too strong to resist or to name, she reached for him.

With the cry of a soul stretched beyond its limits he wrapped his arms around her, dragged her bodily across the little distance that separated them, so that she was pulled half out of her sleeping bag. Then with a muttered word of protest—against her? against his own weakness?—he bent and smothered her mouth with his kiss.

Jalia's heart leaped like a wild animal, twisting and writhing against the cage of her ribs, straining to get into his hand, the strong, hard hand that gripped her ruthlessly and pulled her against him, as if his hands understood her heart's call, were trying to free her heart to love him.

His mouth was fierce against her lips, pressing, chewing, his tongue seeking, his hunger harsh against the soft flesh he desired. With a moan Jalia gave herself up to the assault, her arms clinging, her mouth opening wide to receive his kiss, to give whatever he asked.

Her body raged with a passionate need that distantly amazed her, her blood hot, melted gold, a rich, slow river delivering glowing desire to every part of her, body and soul.

Her breasts sang with delight at the pain of being crushed against his warm chest, at the joy of feeling his heart's wild beating against her body. Her skin shivered and burned as his hands pressed and owned her back, her arms, her neck and face.

His mouth lifted from her mouth and traced over her cheek and chin, then, as her head fell obediently back, down the long line of her throat to the wild pulse at its base.

Then he lifted his head and his hand gripped her upper arm and held her away.

"But my story does not end here," Latif said ruthlessly, and his voice grated with the effort he was now exerting over his own flesh, his blood, his heart, his soul.

"Latif." Jalia moaned her loss in the syllables of his name, a pleading that had never been in her voice before. "Latif, love me, please love me."

He raised his chest, and cool air brushed her. She felt how real the bonds that linked them were, now, because they were being torn as he drew away from her.

"Latif!" She lifted her hands to his face, feeling she would die if she could not hold him and love him.

He caught her wrist and held it tight, too tight, lifting her hand into moonlight.

"Do you ask me to love you with this on your finger?"

The breath rasped in her throat. She had forgotten Michael, forgotten the ring, forgotten everything in the mad sweetness that flooded her.

"Yes!" she cried, for the sweetness still beckoned her on. "Latif, please!" She reached for him again.

"Take it off," he growled, as the tendrils of belonging took advantage of their closeness to enwrap them.

"What?" Jalia pressed a kiss into the little hollow in his shoulder that had been designed for her lips. Drunkenly she thought that she would give anything for the right to kiss his skin just here, all the rest of her life.

"Take off this man's ring. You will marry me. Swear it, and I will love you and you will be mine forever."

So the serpent entered paradise; and she felt its cool silkiness shiver up her heated body, and trembled under the sudden chill of its whispered reasoning.

"What do you mean?" she faltered.

"Do you think I want you for one night, one week, one year, even? You are mine, Jalia. In your heart already you belong to me. Only say it, and I will love you."

An emerald sparkled in a stray moonbeam as his

eyes burned her from the mysterious darkness where his face was. His hands held her tightly, and a part of her thought that she would always be safe in a hold such as this.

"I can't marry you," she protested, and inexplicable tears burned her cheeks.

"Can't?" He repeated the word in a harsh, grating voice, and she saw a flash of white teeth.

"You know I can't. You said it yourself," she accused. "I don't belong here, Latif. It's not my home."

"A woman belongs with her husband. His home is her home. You belong with me. You are Bagestani. Your blood is here. Your heart is here. Your people call to you. I call to you."

His hands tightened on her as the words rained down on her, as if he knew that he had lost. He bent and kissed her again, and fire swept out from the contact of his mouth into her body and soul.

"Answer me," he commanded.

"I want to be your lover," she sobbed. "Please take me as a lover, Latif, and don't ask me for more."

He sat up, his sleeping bag falling down to his hips, exposing his hard-muscled torso to the sharp light and shade of moonlight.

"Are you such a fool as this?" he rasped. "Do you think we can be lovers, and then you will go back and marry that man, and forget what love we had, forget how my body has branded you?

"If I love you, I make you mine! You will be closer to me than my own heart! What shall I do when my heart wishes to leave my body? Do you ask this of me?"

His eyes were black hollows in the harsh shadow

now, his face angled and sharply defined in the moonlight, making him more like a bird of prey than ever.

Her heart twisting with hurt, she drew back from him into the comfortless warmth of her own sleeping bag.

But fear was more powerful than the pain. She knew this was not a question of heart, or even of love: she hadn't known him long enough for that. This was powerful sexual passion, masquerading as love, and she would be ten times worse than a fool to be swayed by it.

Like Noor. Who was now in a downed plane somewhere, paying, perhaps with her life, for a too-long toying with dangerous magic. Was she, who had seen the truth so clearly in Noor's case, going to be blind in her own?

"I'm not Bagestani, Latif," she said, her voice hoarse. "I'm English. We can't change the past. I can't live by your rules."

The look on his star-shadowed face then she knew she would remember all her life long. His jaw clenched and, deft as a wild animal, he slipped away from her side and into the night.

She awoke to sunlight and the sound of cracking wood and turned her head to see Latif on his haunches, the long line of his naked back tucking down into lean hips and thighs as he tended the fire.

He must have hamstrings like elastic bands: he sat easily on the flat of his feet, his butt resting down on his calves, as if the difficult posture were second nature to him.

Watching him now she sensed something that surprised her, because he had always seemed at ease in the city and palace environment: here he was in his true element.

Now she could understand what people meant when they said he was a mountain man. The Sultan had told her that during the long years of working for Ghasib's overthrow, Latif had been his chief liaison with the mountain tribes. The nomadic mountain tribes could not be policed and respected no borders; Latif had slipped in and out of Ghasib's Bagestan at will.

Here she became aware of something she couldn't have named before—his inner silence. He had a capacity for stillness, as if he had learned patience from the mountains. It was deeply attractive.

He was quiet, concentrated, open, like an animal drinking at a spring—as if the mountains were a source of sustenance to him.

And like an animal at a spring, he became aware of her regard, and turned his head. Their eyes met for the first time since he had gone off into the darkness last night. She had fallen asleep without hearing him return.

"Sabah al kheir," he said, in the poetic greeting that was still used in the mountains. *A morning of joy.*

"Sabahan noor," she replied with a smile. *A morning of light.*

And it was. The air was fresh and clear and invigorating, and Jalia accepted the now-familiar jolt of longing for a simpler life, slithered out of her sleeping bag, got up to stretch and yawn luxuriously.

When she recovered, he was watching her with unreadable eyes.

"Yes, you are very beautiful," he said. His voice was a rough, possessive caress, and her flesh moved with that heavy awareness that seemed to be associated with him.

She felt fully in her body now, felt how her breasts sat against her rib cage, felt the mobility of her hips, the length of her own legs. Her skin felt every spot where the cotton of her pyjamas brushed her, felt the elastic snug around her slim waist. How her bare feet were planted on the ground, as if she drew her aliveness from the rock, as much as from the air.

She brought her arms across her breasts, her right hand clasping the opposite shoulder, the left hand under her chin, as she stood looking down at him. Unconsciously she stroked the opals with her thumb.

"Yes," he said, taking the gesture as a protest, "and you are mine, and you do not know it. You do not wish me to say it, but I only tell the truth. You are mine. If you wear another man's ring, even if you marry him, does it change the truth? If it is the truth, nothing can change it.

"We belong together. It is better to say it. My silence was not right. I should have told you in the first moment, when I knew it. Then there would not be this engagement. The fault is mine."

Jalia would have denied everything, if only she could have trusted herself to speak. Sensation was running over and through her, half indignation, half melting response. If she opened her mouth to speak, could she know which half would get the microphone?

The mountain man turned back to his task with the fire, and Jalia picked up her toiletry bag, towel and clothes and slipped off up the slope to her morning scrub.

So there were going to be no reproaches over what had happened last night. Latif was, apparently, a man not inclined to sulking when he didn't get what he wanted, and as she washed in the icy little mountain stream, gasping with the shock, she thought of how it would be to have such a man for a husband.

Most of the men she dated sulked, one way or another, if they didn't get their own way. As if they had never quite got over some disappointment with their mothers.

Latif was a man who could, it seemed, accept setback as a part of life, not—as with so many of the men she knew, including Michael—as something someone had done to him.

Her father had always said the mountain men of Bagestan were a breed apart. Maybe you had to come to the mountains to get a real man. If you wanted one. Jalia didn't. Anyway, it was too late for her. To have a man like Latif as husband, she should have been here from birth, for how could she ever fit in to this culture and life, growing up the way she had in the bustle and freedom of a world-class city?

She wasn't sorry, not really. She belonged in another world, when if history had been different she might have belonged in this one, and that, too, was just life.

But a part of her, she realized as she rubbed herself down with the rough towel, trying to get warm again after her chilly dip—a little part of her was sorry to think that she would never experience Latif's real passion.

And she did wonder if she would always remember Latif's passionate proposal as the moment of wildest romantic thrill of her life. How could any Western man match it?

She dressed and returned down the slope to the evocative smell of coffee and wood smoke.

Latif had draped two round flat pieces of *naan* over the spit, and when he handed one to her it was toasted and deliciously flavoured with the fat of last night's meat it had absorbed from the spit.

She spread some goat's cheese on the bread and rolled it up for a simple, succulent breakfast.

"Where to this morning?" she asked, for something to say.

"I want to go down into the valley. It is a journey on foot, since the road has been washed out in many places. Do you want to come with me, or wait for me here?"

Jalia hesitated. "How long will it take?"

"If I go alone, a few hours. If you come with me, longer."

Maybe it was his arrogant assumption that she would slow him down, or maybe just a reluctance to sit here doing nothing, she wasn't sure. But with a little flick of her head that made him smile, Jalia opted to accompany him.

Nine

Arrogant or not, he had been speaking nothing but the truth. Latif went over the deep gullies the rains had gouged into the road with an ease and a balance that terrified her, while Jalia could only inch her way with his help.

When they came to a terrifying drop, an ugly, massive gouge in the road that fell away to nothing, he took her piggyback, and the sheer power and strength beneath her knees had a rhythmic, muscled beauty that carried to her animal brain a deep, pure erotic message, so that her legs' sudden tightening around him caused him to lose his hold for a second, almost pulling them to their doom.

On the road again her body was lazily reluctant to get down.

Panting with the aftermath of sharp fear and sudden

desire, Jalia straightened her clothes fussily, irritated with herself for that uncontrolled response. If she didn't get a grip, she'd find herself married to the man, for no better reason than to experience his love-making.

A truth suddenly dawned on her, as stunning as a clap of thunder—every time she had argued with Noor about her foolish attraction to Bari, she had been talking to herself. She might not have allowed the information into conscious awareness, but unconsciously she had recognized how wildly attracted she was to Latif.

What a fool she had been, blind and smug: because if she had allowed herself to see the real problem, she could have taken much smarter action to avoid Latif.

And she wouldn't be where she was right now— dependent on him for her survival, and hoping against hope that he would crack and make love to her before she cracked and promised him whatever price he asked.

"Why won't you make love to me?" she asked, before she could stop herself, as they picked their way past the boulders strewn in the road.

Latif glanced at her without surprise, so he must have felt that deep connection, too. "I will," he said.

"Oh!" She couldn't stop the smile that played over her mouth, nor the delighted surge of anticipation in her blood, and as if he were powerless in the face of such evidence of her desire, his arms went around her and he pulled her against him.

Fire burned up around her, and with a gasp she parted her lips and tilted her chin to invite his kiss.

"When you have my ring on your finger instead

of the one you now wear,'' he continued, and then his lips came down on hers with a power of masculine demand that sent sensation whipping into every nerve.

Her arms wrapped him, her body fitted against his as he bent her back over his arm, twined his fingers into her hair, and the hard, pushing response of his arousal pressed against her to produce a fierce melting that buckled her knees like butter on a stove.

Her head was caught in the crook of one arm, his other hand was hot and hard against the back of her waist, and she felt how easy it would be for him to overwhelm her, because he was strong, much stronger than she had guessed, and her blood soared with the knowledge.

He lifted his mouth and stared at her from green eyes almost black with need. She had never seen so deep a green, and she could have stayed there all day just exploring the magic of that emerald pitch, that glinting hunger, feeling her danger and her safety in his hold, feeling how the world held its breath.

''It will be difficult,'' he admitted, with a hoarse exhalation. ''Which of us will be the winner?''

Jalia took a deep, calming breath. It was impossible to make love here on the road, but she had lost track of time and place while his mouth was on hers.

Around the next mound of fallen rock they met a team working to mend the road. With only manpower and a couple of donkeys they were gathering up the rocks that had come down from the ridge above and were packing them into the gullies that the rains had gouged: backbreaking, dangerous work, but the men and boys seemed cheerful enough.

When Latif and Jalia appeared suddenly on the

road they all looked up and gave the Bagestani greeting of a fist to the heart. A moment later someone recognized Latif.

"You come in a good time, Lord!" they cried in formal greeting.

"May your shadow never grow less!"

"You come to sit on the council, Lord?" said another anxiously. "I have a petition…."

No one kowtowed to him, Jalia saw, though he was the man they called their *Shahin*: they had too much self-respect, it seemed. Between Latif and the men there was a mutual exchange of respect. And yet it was clear they would accept his judgement.

After a few moments Latif said, "I escort the Princess Jalia on a search for her cousin, Princess Noor," and explained about the downed plane for the fiftieth time since they had begun this quest.

She exchanged nods with the men. In her jeans and desert boots and shirt, she must have been a somewhat unusual sight, but none of them stared at her, a fact she was getting used to after so many days in the mountains.

As her father had told her in endless stories during her childhood, the mountain people of Bagestan were a ferociously proud people, but they were also hospitable and polite, and they would never stare at a strange woman.

Some of the conversation that now ensued was too quick for her to follow, more so since several people were talking at once, but she understood that no one had seen or heard anything resembling a plane in trouble or crashing.

Then it seemed they were urging Latif to remain

in the valley for a day or two to sit with the village council for some important cases. After a while, one man left the team and accompanied Latif and Jalia down the mountain.

The man led them to his own house, where his wife and daughters smilingly produced lunch for them. As usual, they ate in silence, and it wasn't till after the meal was over that Latif said, "There are several urgent matters before the council. It's important that I sit to hear them. But it means that we will not leave the valley tonight."

Jalia nodded her acceptance of the situation.

"Some of the younger boys will go and bring what you need from the truck. What do you need?"

"Only my backpack."

Later, while the members of the council gathered at one of the houses in the village, greeting Latif with loud welcome, the women led Jalia up the hillside to an isolated house set in a walled, terraced garden, whose profusion of flowers and greenery she had noticed from their campsite this morning.

"What house be this?" she asked in her archaic, textbook Bagestani.

"Lady Jalia, this is the home of your future husband." The women smiled. "If you do not know it now, you will soon be familiar with it, if God wills!"

Jalia's smile stiffened a little. This was a dilemma, for if she denied being Latif's fiancée, she would have to be housed somewhere else. She knew enough of the country traditions to understand that.

And she didn't want to sleep anywhere else; she wanted to sleep with Latif. Was she going to turn her back on the possibility that he had cracked, that he had decided to make love to her?

Not a chance. And if this arrangement left Latif in future explaining to his tribe just why Princess Jalia did not return to the valley as his bride, that was his problem, wasn't it?

So in the split second she had to choose, Jalia chose to say nothing. The women smiled and nodded and led her inside.

"The ways of the outside world are strange," one of them observed on a note of laughter. "Here in the valley no man takes his bride to his home before the ceremony has been concluded. How will you negotiate a good dowry, Lady Jalia, if you give up your jewel to his keeping before he pays for it?"

"Even a noble lord like Lord Latif—do not all men dream of capturing a woman's prize, giving nothing in return?"

"For shame, Amina! When a man like Lord Latif declares himself before witnesses, that is as good as a marriage contract!"

They were laughing the way women laugh who are leading the bride to her new husband's bed, and to her amazed dismay, Jalia felt her cheeks growing warm.

"When the time comes, Lady Jalia, will you come to the valley, and let us marry you?" asked one young, pretty woman who, it was obvious from certain joking comments, was only recently married herself.

"Foolish Parvana! The ceremony will take place in the palace, of course...."

So the laughter and banter went on, while the

women showed her around the pleasant house and garden that was Latif's family home. It was bigger than many in the village, but not out of scale: it had two domes, when many of the houses it overlooked had only one, and a very large enclosed garden, and a high wall.

"Because in times of trouble the women and children of the valley came here with the animals," someone explained. "Then the chief and the men would ride out to fight."

"When Ghasib's men came, we did not fight. We had heard that it was more dangerous to fight. Once the tunnel was built, we knew, he could bring as many soldiers as he needed...."

"Many of the treasures of this house were buried, Lady Jalia," someone explained, pointing to the bare walls and floors and niches. "That is how we protected ourselves from Ghasib's looting. We knew that his men would steal all our treasures if they saw them. We hid and buried many, and left out only a few, so that they would not be suspicious. That is why the house is so empty. Do not fear that Ghasib got the treasures of our Shahin."

"No, the earth holds them!"

That seemed to be a joke, too, but no one explained, and with so much going on, and the language so difficult for her, Jalia let it go.

"We had word that Lord Latif would come, but not that he brought his bride! Look how the chamber is not decorated, Lady Jalia, but we will bring perfumes and lamps...."

She didn't protest. Why shouldn't they set up the bedroom for seduction, though they completely misunderstood who would be seduced and who seducer?

Ten

The women, young and old, began the ritual decoration of the bedchamber.

It seemed as if, in order to cope with this invasion of outside moral laxity, they had simply decided to rewrite the agenda. Lord Latif had said that he intended to marry the Princess—therefore he had married her. This was their wedding night.

So the afternoon was spent preparing and bringing special foods for the couple, and creating a bed of flowers and scented boughs, in the ancient tradition, and enacting a few other little rituals that Jalia knew her colleague at university, whose field was the early history of the area, would give his eyeteeth to watch.

Someone gave her beautifully embroidered pyjamas to wear, in soft jade silk, the trousers caught at the ankles, the jacket closed over the breasts with one delicate embroidery frog. Jalia knew it must be something that had been worked on and treasured up for the girl's own wedding, but they insisted, and it was impossible to refuse the gift. All she could do was make a mental promise to herself to find something as beautiful to send back to the valley as soon as she returned to al Bostan.

They bathed her, and rubbed her skin with a curious perfumed salve, and plaited special love knots into her hair, though grieving that it wasn't long enough, not even to the shoulders!—how strange things must be in the outside world, if a woman voluntarily cut off her own glory!

They marvelled at the paleness of her hair, straight and almost white, when every woman in the valley had black, thick curls. Just so, they had sometimes heard, was the hair of the Kamrangi tribeswomen, a marvel someone's grandfather had seen many years ago, when he had accompanied some foreigner as guide into many strange places...

Jalia was falling more and more under the spell of the women and their beautiful valley. Their values were plain and true, their laughter infectious, their collective beauty and wisdom astounding. Whenever she tried to claw back a sense of her own world, it rang false in this pure environment, like a toxin in the fresh mountain air.

She mentioned, for example, the village council that was sitting—weren't the women annoyed that they were not members, that they didn't decide such matters along with the men?

There were smiles and shrugs all around the circle—yes, it was true that in the ancient days in the valley the council had been all women instead of all men, and that was as it should be, for women were much better judges of human nature than men, and everyone knew it.

But men were good judges of the law. Most petitions to the council now were legal matters—who owned a piece of land, who was entitled to inherit—and were both uninteresting and unimportant, though of course the men could not be expected to think so.

The serious work of the tribe—who should marry whom, for example, and when, decisions about planting and harvest and festivals—was still carried on by the women.

And eventually Jalia simply gave up trying to connect the two worlds, and enjoyed being with the women and seeing life from their point of view.

When the sun was setting beyond the walls of the beautiful but neglected garden, their work finished, the women declared that the council would have broken up by now. They left Jalia in the lamp-lighted, sweet-scented bedroom, wearing the silky jade tunic and trousers, and went off, promising to send Latif to her.

And within the hour he was there, bathed, oiled and perfumed in his turn, and wearing a white outfit, beautifully embroidered, whose flowing silk only underlined his powerful masculinity.

He was unbelievably gorgeous as he entered the room, a bemused smile playing over his dark falcon's face.

He stood for a moment looking down at her in the soft shadows cast by the candle lamps, and Jalia's heart leaped at the expression that came into his eyes—possessive and hungry and determined.

With a curious shifting the atmosphere grew thick around them, and he gazed at her with green eyes gone black, a signal her body already understood directly. It responded with melting hunger, and she tossed her head in the way he knew so well, pressed her lips together, and let her eyes smile at him.

"The…the women left food for you," she murmured.

But he didn't hear. He was gazing at her, smelling her, almost tasting her across the room.

She was hauntingly beautiful now, in the traditional bridal robes of his tribe, which breathed across her body, hiding and revealing the curve and length, the softness and strength of her. Her hair was woven with flowers and shimmer, her skin oiled and scented, so that the least move announced itself to his desperately hungry senses.

His woman, prepared as a bride is prepared, in silks and perfumes, her eyes kohled and inviting, prepared as he had longed to see her since that first moment of glancing into cool slate-green eyes…

In two strides he was across the room, and he lifted his hands to cup her head and hold her face up, a flower, a perfect flower with two wide green centres so full of sweetness that his heart stopped.

"You are mine," he said, his voice rough with feeling. "You have promised. You have told the women."

Before she could protest that it was not so, he bent his head, and tenderly, tastingly, his mouth stroked hers, as a man might kiss a delicate bloom, to absorb its perfume through his lips.

The touch trembled against her mouth, and a thousand nerve endings sent shimmers of delight all through her. She shivered, and her lips parted. Her hands pressed his shoulders, and his mouth moved more and more hungrily against her, seeking the sweetness it tasted, as if the more he tasted, the more his need was fed.

Then his hand slipped under the silken shirt she wore, and she felt its heat and strength push along the length of her back, drawing her slowly, determinedly in against his body in a curving arc as he bent over her, lifting her almost off her feet. Her head he wrapped in the crook of his other arm, and she lay supported in his embrace, breast to breast, mouth to mouth.

With the flick of his thumb her jacket fell open, and he stroked her stomach, her chest, her breasts.

From every contact honeyed electricity poured through her, body and soul, setting fire to her mind, igniting her blood. Fever burned her, the fever of a deep hunger that was all new to her. When he lifted his mouth, his eyes, black with passion and intent, devoured her with answering hunger, and her throat of its own accord murmured its need.

With a directness that shook her, his hand left her back and moved between her thighs, and the million nerve endings there leaped to obedient awareness, and she swooned.

She lay helplessly arced in the air, supported between her feet on the floor and her head in his arm, and his mouth kissed her lips, her ear, her throat, while his other hand slid to her waist and unerringly found the tie of the pyjama trousers. Then she felt the whisper of silk over her stomach and down her thighs, and a moment later her lower body was naked and exposed. A sense of her own vulnerability charged through her.

He lifted his mouth from its exploration of her throat to look down at her body, and the expression on his face poured fuel on the fire of her hunger so that she gasped, and when his hand cupped her mound with possessive firmness, the small gasp was overtaken by a hoarse cry of surprise, hunger, and anticipation. Then she submitted to her own openness, to her vulnerable nakedness, to her admission of sexual hunger.

His hand moved unerringly against her thighs, drawing them apart to give him better access, and then returned to the soft nest of his intent. His hand clasped her again, and his eyes burned into hers, as if to declare his right to do so. Then, hot and sensuously tormenting, it began to move against the nested, humming nerves that waited there.

Under his rhythmic stroking a burning heat quickly built up in her, and she pressed hungrily against him, arching, tensing and seeking, until the pleasure burst under his touch, like a rivulet of lava whispering down a mountain slope.

Her thighs trembled, her breasts tightened, all her body awoke to song.

"Oh!" she cried softly. "Thank you!"

She sighed and tried to straighten, but he kept her there, kept his hand where it was, still moving, so that

GET FREE BOOKS and a FREE GIFT WHEN YOU PLAY THE...

Lucky 7

Just scratch off the silver box with a coin. Then check below to see the gifts you get!

SLOT MACHINE GAME!

YES! I have scratched off the silver box. Please send me the 2 free Silhouette Desire® books and gift for which I qualify. I understand I am under no obligation to purchase any books, as explained on the back of this card.

326 SDL D353   **225 SDL D36K**

FIRST NAME

LAST NAME

ADDRESS

APT.#   CITY

STATE/PROV.   ZIP/POSTAL CODE

7	7	7	Worth TWO FREE BOOKS plus a BONUS Mystery Gift!
🍒	🍒	🍒	Worth TWO FREE BOOKS!
♣	♣	♣	Worth ONE FREE BOOK!
🔔	🔔	🍒	TRY AGAIN!

www.eHarlequin.com

(S-D-12/04)

The Silhouette Reader Service™ — Here's how it works:

Accepting your 2 free books and gift places you under no obligation to buy anything. You may keep the books and gift and return the shipping statement marked "cancel." If you do not cancel, about a month later we'll send you 6 additional books and bill you just $3.80 each in the U.S., or $4.47 each in Canada, plus 25¢ shipping and handling per book and applicable taxes if any.* That's the complete price and — compared to cover prices of $4.50 each in the U.S. and $5.25 each in Canada — it's quite a bargain! You may cancel at any time, but if you choose to continue, every month we'll send you 6 more books, which you may either purchase at the discount price or return to us and cancel your subscription.
*Terms and prices subject to change without notice. Sales tax applicable in N.Y. Canadian residents will be charged applicable provincial taxes and GST. Credit or debit balances in a customer's account(s) may be offset by any other outstanding balance owed by or to the customer.

If offer card is missing write to: Silhouette Reader Service, 3010 Walden Ave., P.O. Box 1867, Buffalo NY 14240-1867

BUSINESS REPLY MAIL
FIRST-CLASS MAIL   PERMIT NO. 717-003   BUFFALO, NY

POSTAGE WILL BE PAID BY ADDRESSEE

SILHOUETTE READER SERVICE
3010 WALDEN AVE
PO BOX 1867
BUFFALO NY 14240-9952

NO POSTAGE
NECESSARY
IF MAILED
IN THE
UNITED STATES

the burst of pleasure was overtaken by the promise of more.

"Do you thank me for so little?" he asked hoarsely. His eyes glowed the deepest green she had ever seen, and he smiled his falcon smile, hungry and intent. "There is more than this, I think."

A moment later, more pleasure zinged out from under his touch, shivering through her so that her back arched, and her hands gripped his shoulders. Her eyes squeezed shut, as if to concentrate on the path the liquid heat was taking through her blood.

Now her legs opened wider of their own accord, her feet planting on the floor, and he saw what he had wanted to see—an unashamed demand for her body's delight. He bent his head and devoured her mouth with his kiss, the better to taste the pleasure as it sang through her again.

"Oh!" Jalia whispered when he lifted his mouth again. "Doesn't it stop?"

He smiled. "No, Beloved. It doesn't stop."

He watched her face for the marks of the delight he gave her as he stroked her body, and sometimes he watched her body, and she saw the marks of her pleasure on his own face.

She had never before met such blatant determination to create sexual satisfaction for her, such open intent. Never had she felt so free to demand and enjoy her body's bliss. Never had she been so lost to her surroundings, her awareness limited to her body, his touch. Never had she felt she might faint with sheer sexual joy.

Her cries shuddered to the ceiling again, and then for a moment the stroking stopped and her hand was drawn into the light to expose the trio of opals on her finger.

Dark, dark eyes came close to hers, and even that was somehow lost in the haze. As was his voice.

You still wear his ring?

"Oh!" she cried softly.

She felt his fingers clasp her finger, felt electricity jolting through her.

Tell me to take it off. Tell me you break this engagement.

She half smiled, her mind reeling, for he had truly made her drunk with pleasure. "I can't do that," she murmured.

His dark frown came between her and the light. *Not? Shall I stop loving you, my Jalia, my woman, my wife? Shall I let you go to this man, my perfect bride?*

"Because we were never engaged," she continued dreamily, only dimly aware that she was throwing away her most potent armour and now nothing would protect her from the fierce wind of his love. "We just pretended, so I'd be safe. Michael's a friend at the university."

She felt the ring leave her finger, felt it in the burning stroke of his fingers as they drew it off her supersensitized skin, heard it bounce from a carpet and skitter across the tiled floor, and then she was falling.

Down, down he dragged her, to that sweet-smelling bed of boughs and blossoms so lovingly created by the women. His kisses grew wild and wilder, over her face, her throat, her ear, back to her swollen, starving mouth. •

Now he stripped off her shirt, exposing her breasts

to the warm lamplight, and slipped out of the white silk that hid his dark body from her hungry gaze. He knelt between her thighs, his eyes moving over her beautiful body as his hands did, creating burning delight in their wake; and where he stroked, he knew her, and where he knew, he owned.

She shuddered as desire abruptly made the leap to passion in her, and groaning, she reached hungrily to pull him into the hot, moist nest of need between her thighs.

He resisted for a moment, and placed his mouth there instead, and as his strong tongue drove her higher up the peak of pleasure, with a last release of the invisible bonds that had constrained her, Jalia twined her fingers into his hair and pressed him against her flesh. His mouth obeyed, a rush of paralysing pleasure engulfed her, and she cried out with utter abandon and fell back against the bower spent and exhausted.

Then he knelt between her legs again, and she saw the engine of his own pleasure, hugely engorged, push its way into her body. Dimly she felt there was nothing more to give or to feel. But her throat opened on a high wild cry, for a deeper pleasure invaded her being now, and the promise of yet more.

She never afterwards knew how much time passed in that scented ecstasy of passion, with Latif's hands and mouth and body stroking her, body and soul, and calling up the deepest, most charged pleasure of all her life. There was a thrilling passion in every part of her being, a yearning and a delight, so that she lost track not merely of time, but of herself, not knowing where she ended and lamplight began, where she ended and pleasure began, where she ended and Latif began....

It was passion, and joy, and soaring, utter perfection. And now a roaring, burning pleasure began to build in her, unlike anything that had come before. She cried and whimpered, and moaned and called to him, as it built to a crescendo in them both, and his voice crying out his own hot urgency added to her delight.

Then she understood that the trickles and rivulets and rivers of heat and delight that came before had been only the foretaste of a deeper, richer, unimagined joy. And now it erupted in and through them both, as if they two—body and soul—were the conduit by which joy and delight and happiness and perfect union burst into the world to feed the starving multitudes.

And so Latif Abd al Razzaq Shahin took his beloved and made her his wife.

Eleven

Later she lay across his dark, damp chest and felt how right it was that she should be there. The memory of pleasure still coursed through her, so that small aftershocks shook her from time to time.

She lifted her head and gazed down into eyes that glowed back at her with satisfied fulfillment at having given and received so much deep pleasure.

After a moment, he picked up her left hand. His thumb stroked her ring finger.

"You were not really engaged to this man?"

"Michael was my insurance policy. My armour against—my parents," she admitted. She couldn't say *against you.*

"How does a man pretend to be engaged to a woman like you, and not wish to make it real?" he wondered softly. "It is not possible. This was a tactic he used. He will want to hold you to it."

She smiled, because the look in his eyes was intoxicating, and shook her head.

"No, it's not like that. Michael's gay. He hasn't come out to his parents yet. I sometimes go to their family parties and things as his date, because he says he likes to keep his mother happy. So when I needed the return favour..."

He looked as though he hardly believed her, but the smile on his face betokened ill for Michael if what she said was not the truth. Jalia's voice faded into silence as she suddenly realized she might have taken powerful forces too lightly.

"I hope what you say is true," Latif said in a rough whisper.

She faltered. "Wh-what?"

"I will hold you, Jalia," he promised. "I will keep you. You are my woman, and so it has always been."

Just for one treacherous second she half wished this moment *could* seal her fate, the way he intended, the way it would have done if life had been different. Just here, and just now, she half believed it might.

It couldn't, but she wasn't going to let reality in yet. Tonight was dreamtime. Tomorrow was soon enough to awaken.

"There's some really delicious food over there," she murmured. "Are you hungry?"

One dark hand stroked her, and, exhausted as she was, her body sang another chorus for him. "For the food of my valley I am always hungry," he said. "Just as I shall always be hungry for you, as long as I live."

Her heart kicked a response so deep she felt tears burn her eyelids, but she smiled and lifted herself away from him. She stood naked in the soft, gentle light, and his gaze in its golden glow felt like honey on her skin—sweet, warm, sensuous.

"Come, then," she said, for the food was laid out to keep warm on a brazier beside piles of embroidered cushions, artfully arranged by the experts of the valley's wedding team.

They both pulled on the silk trousers of their outfits, and sank down again on the cushions, he looking like a genie sprung from one of the antique lamps, she like a dancing girl, her bare breasts glowing with the mix of oil and love-sweat.

Roasted eggplant in olive oil, spiced meats, yogurt and garlic, fresh herbs with goat's cheese, and a delicious pan-fried bread...nothing in her life had ever tasted so delicious, or so potently aphrodisiac, as this meal.

With smiles and lazy eyes they ate, and murmured appreciation both of this feast and of the one just past, fed each other morsels and tidbits, and, mouths shiny with spiced oil, licked each other's lips, and their own.

"The women around here certainly know how to cook," Jalia exclaimed once, a little breathlessly, as one such lip licking turned into a spice-flavoured kiss.

"The dishes of the Marzuqi are known through all the countries bordering the Gulf of Barakat," he said. They talked a little about the food they ate, while their eyes carried other messages, some lazy and slow, some electric with promise.

Once she gestured to the empty walls and niches of the room.

"One of the women—Golnesar, I think—said

something about the treasures of the valley having been hidden from Ghasib's men, and they all laughed, as if that was a joke. But no one explained.''

He smiled. ''You know what a taste Ghasib had for ancient art treasures.''

Jalia nodded. One of Latif's tasks had been to help her parents trace and reclaim family heirlooms grabbed by Ghasib or his minions in the years of the republic. They had looted in the name of the country's museums, but most of the treasures went into Ghasib's personal treasury.

''We all knew what it meant when the tunnel was being blasted through the rock to make way for Ghasib's road—first through would be Ghasib's acquisition team. There were many treasures decorating the homes of the valley, some of inestimable historical value.

''My father made the decision to prevent the stripping of the valley. He instructed the people to bring their treasures to him, and said that he would personally hide them all in a secret location.''

''Wouldn't it have been safer to have dozens of hiding places, so if they found one the others would still be safe?''

''Recollect that Ghasib had ways to extract information from people. Once he learned that one village or family had hidden something, no one in the valley would have been safe. This way, if Ghasib's men suspected a trick, under duress everyone could honestly say that they had been ordered to give up their treasures to the Shahin, and knew nothing more.''

''And your father would be the one who was tortured,'' Jalia suggested.

"Exactly. But he believed that the secret would be better kept if all knew that their Shahin's life hung in the balance, and he was right. Ghasib's men took the valuables that had been left in a few homes to allay suspicion, and never got a hint of the truth."

Jalia frowned. "And why haven't the treasures been brought out of hiding since the Sultan's return?"

"Because my father hid the treasures too well. Only he and a very old and trusted servant knew the location. He deliberately chose an old man—*If they torture us, we will die quickly,* he said. Pir Gholam died soon after, and my father, sadly, also died before Ash's plans succeeded. Just before his death he told me he had left directions for me, but I haven't found those directions."

Jalia laughed. "Have you any idea where the hiding place might be?"

"None. But I have been absent so much, there has been little time to conduct a search, even through my father's papers. When work with Ash eases off, and there is more time for the valley's concerns, I will embark on a systematic search."

His expression was completely open and true, and Jalia experienced a sharp jolt of culture shock. In the West, she thought, his father would have come under immediate suspicion of having stolen or sold off his people's treasures, and his son would be anxious to avert that suspicion.

But in Latif's face there was no awareness that such a suspicion might enter her mind or anyone else's. He trusted in his father's probity, and therefore in his own. And so, clearly, did his people.

"Now I see why they call your family the Third Shahin," she murmured.

He frowned quizzically. "Yes?"

"This afternoon I asked the women how the valley got its name," Jalia explained.

"And what did they tell you?"

"Sey-Shahin. Three Royal Falcons," Jalia said, unconsciously settling into the role of storyteller, as if she had been born in the valley herself.

"They said that in very ancient times, this valley was a plain. It was fertile, but because it was so flat, the wind used to blow over it, taking their seed before it had rooted, and carrying off the rich soil.

"So the people sent a messenger to the Great King—some say to God—and in reply the Great King sent his favourite royal falcon to stand guard over the valley, and protect it from the winds.

"And the falcon stood so long, and guarded them so loyally, that he became a mountain, and still stands guard now.

"But the people were still troubled, for the floodwaters came down from the mountains in spring, and because there was nothing to stop them, they flowed through the valley, carrying with them the seed before it could sprout, and the rich soil.

"So the people sent another messenger to the Great King, and he sent a second of his royal falcons, to guard the valley against the floodwaters. And the falcon stood guard so loyally that he became rock, and he is the mountain on the south.

"And the valley prospered with its two mountain guardians, but the people began to worry, for there was trouble in the lands, and a great conqueror was on the move.

"Then the people sent to God a third time, begging for protection from the invader, and God sent a third royal falcon—a great leader. And the leader reigned a long time, and protected them so well that his family became a rock for the people of the valley, and every generation produces a strong, able leader to protect them.

"They are called the Shahini, The People of the Falcon, and they will be leaders in the valley till the time comes for the valley to be destroyed. That's you, and they are so proud of you and your family, Latif."

Latif watched her from under drooping eyelids. "And what else?"

"So the valley was protected from the winds, and the floods, and from foreign conquerors, but there was still one thing that was not protected, and that was the hearts of the people.

"So the people asked God for protection for their hearts, and God sent the fourth and last protection— he sent them Islam. And now the valley is protected in all four directions, and no harm can come to the people, and that's why they are now called al Marzuqi, the Blessed, the Provided For," she finished, smiling.

"Did I get it right? It's a lovely story."

"You tell it well. One day, if God wills, you will tell it to our children."

She could only press her lips together and shake her head.

When they had finished the meal with fresh fruit, they washed hands and mouths with rose-scented water poured each for the other from the intricately moulded silver ewer with its matching bowl.

Then Latif lifted the trays and brazier to one side and Jalia lay back on the cushions, feeling crazily free and unlike herself in bare breasts and harem pants.

He lay down again and rested on one elbow beside her, gazing into her eyes in a way that made her body remember delight.

He drew out a tiny white flower that still lurked in a twist of her hair, lazily touched it to the end of his nose, inhaled like a man tasting fine wine, and, watching her with a look in his eyes that she would never forget, thoughtfully caught it on the end of his tongue, drew it into his mouth, and ate it.

Jalia's throat gave a little involuntary whimper of reaction and she lost track of what she was saying.

Latif lay back on the cushions and drew her onto his chest. Her breasts brushed hungrily against the mat of hair, and her hips melted with renewed yearning as his strong hand stroked down her back and over the swell of her bottom, lightly, possessively.

"Why did the women do all this?" she asked, nodding at the now empty trays and the room. "They know we aren't married."

"They tell me that the date is very auspicious for the wedding of the Shahin. There won't be another such beneficial day for months, or maybe years, according to the old way of reckoning such things."

Jalia frowned curiously. "What is the old way of reckoning such things?"

"Only the women know."

"Do you believe them?"

He shrugged. "It was predicted to me last year that

this year would be beneficial for our attempts to put Ash on the throne. They also said that if the Sultan returned the drought would end."

"Pretty impressive. But we aren't married, so how can it be beneficial just to decorate a bedroom?"

Latif smiled. "By the rules of the old, pre-Islamic tradition, we are married. This is all it takes, that bride and groom should be bathed and perfumed and led to bed by the women."

"What?" She leaped as if from an electric shock, and Latif laughed.

"The ritual allowed the women of the tribe to make sure that bride and groom had the necessary parts in good working order. Some parts of the ritual have been abandoned since Islam came to the valley—the groom used to be put through his paces by the women, they say.

"But the practice itself has never been wholly abandoned. Tradition is a powerful thing, and most people here would not feel married without this."

He toyed with another lock of hair, twirled another flower, smiled at her. "They didn't explain this to you?"

"No. They just—started stripping me off. Latif…what will you say when you come back to the valley and I'm not with you?"

He didn't move, didn't flinch. But she saw something hit him, all the same.

"What does man do when he loses what is most precious to him?" he asked, his voice raw. "I will tell them the truth. That I could not hold my woman, even though the world is black for me without her."

Twelve

In the morning the council sat again, while Jalia was taken around all the houses in the village and introduced to children and pet goats. The women began to tell her of their lives and their problems, laughing with delight to hear her formal, archaic speech.

Bagestani Arabic was not the first language of the mountain tribes, and most people still spoke Parvani by preference, but even so they were all—even the oldest women—a whole lot more fluent than Jalia.

It didn't take Jalia long to understand what was going on—they were petitioning her interest as the wife of the Shahin. In this way they hoped to bring their problems to his attention.

Jalia began to deeply regret that she hadn't told the villagers at once that she was not going to marry their leader.

But she was also a cousin of the Sultan, she reflected after a moment. She could still be of use. So she listened as patiently as if she had been Latif's bride, after all.

Late in the morning, when she had been offered tea and a plateful of delicious little delicacies she couldn't resist, she was invited to visit the village's "carpet room."

"Indeed, it would honour me to make such a visit," the Princess said, making the young girls giggle again, and repeat her archaic speech. But there was no malice in their delight, and no one scolded them.

So they took her to a house where she was surprised to see a circle of hand looms. In honour of Latif and Jalia's visit, no one was working at them, but that it was a busy place when it got going was evident in the beautiful carpets partly finished on many looms and the stacks of coloured thread around the room.

Predominant among the clusters of wool and silk was a mountain of beautiful purple-blue thread, rich and luxurious, a unique colour; and with a gasp Jalia bent over the nearest loom.

"Marzuqi carpets!" she exclaimed in English. She hadn't made the connection before, but anyone with an interest in Eastern carpets would have recognized the distinctive colour and design at once.

Marzuqi carpets were extremely sought after, very expensive, and hard to come by, and Princess Muna had treasured the one she owned all of Jalia's life. But Jalia had simply not made the connection until it was right before her eyes.

"My honoured mother, the Princess Muna, hath of such carpets as these one carpet which she treasures greatly," she told them. "They are carpets among the most beautiful carpets in the world."

Of course this pleased them, but like a fool Jalia hadn't thought of the consequences. She was immediately presented with a silk carpet just finished, the result of at least a year's work on the part of one of the women, she knew: far too costly a gift.

She was sure that the carpet had been made to order for some client, yet it would be impossible to refuse without offence.

With a sinking heart totally at variance with her delight in the carpet, Jalia examined the intricate design, the beautifully woven pattern a mix of several intensities of the blue, accented with black, white, pink and green.

"This is a sacred pattern, Lady," she was told. "It is designed to draw Truth into the space. These are secrets handed down to us from our mothers since The Days Before the Law of Men."

The Days Before the Law of Men. It was a strange phrase, one she had never heard before, and yet it had the ring of common usage. She bent over the gorgeous carpet, listening while they explained how the meaning of the signs and markings had a deep mystery that could not be explained in words.

Afterwards, they folded the carpet up and tied it for her. Jalia made her thanks, but tried to protest that the client for whom this carpet had been intended would be angry.

"But it has been made for Lord Latif, against the day when he would appear!" they exclaimed. "Razan is the valley's best weaver—who else to weave a carpet for your husband? We are honoured to give it to you. You will take it to the city, so that there you and Lord Latif will be always reminded of your true home.''

Jalia didn't understand why that brought tears to her eyes. The valley was not her home, and it never could be. She had gone too far away from such roots. But still, some part of her yearned for the might-have-been.

After lunch, some of the men escorted Latif and Jalia back up the slowly mending road to their truck, loaded it with the carpet and fresh supplies, and waved them on their way.

As they drove, Jalia did not wait long before broaching the chief subject of concern that the women had raised with her: a problem that threatened their livelihood and the future of the entire valley.

''They've got two problems,'' she explained. ''The first is, the exporter of their carpets, with whom they have a contract to sell everything they produce, has started having cheap, production-line copies made in Kaljukistan, and is trying to pass them off as genuine.

''He says the women aren't producing fast enough to fulfill demand, but the truth is, he wants cheap carpets to sell to people who can't afford the genuine thing.

''But he's got a problem—he can't achieve the colour with chemical dyes, and you know the colour is half the beauty of a Marzuqi carpet. So now he's trying to force them to give him the secret of that wonderful purple-blue dye. It really beggars belief. It's just ruthless profiteering without any—''

Latif interrupted. "But this could be a good thing for the women. Tastes change. Maybe they should profit from the demand for their designs while they can.''

Jalia turned to stare at him. "Latif—handwoven Marzuqi carpets have been hot in the West for the past hundred years at least. That's not going to change as long as they keep it small and exclusive. It will certainly change if the market gets flooded with cheap copies and it becomes the latest craze.''

"They aren't going to lose their skill in making carpets. All they have to do is find new designs.''

She couldn't believe it. She had been so certain of being able to enlist his help.

"I thought these were your people, Latif," she cried. "They need help!''

"Do they?''

"In the last contract the exporter tied them up without their realizing it. They can't sell to anyone but him, but he's not obliged to buy what they produce if there's no market.

"He's saying the carpets are too expensive, and take too long to make. He says there's no market beyond the carpets already ordered. Those carpets will all be finished within six months.

"After that—the prices they are being offered are less than half of what they now get, which is already obscenely exploitative. And the agent wants to bring in a designer, so that instead of creating their own variations on their designs as they go, the women just execute a preexisting design. That's supposed to make the work go faster.

"The women all hate the idea. Each carpet is unique, an individual work of art. With a preset design they'll be just technicians. They'll have no creative input at all."

"What help do they want?"

"Isn't it obvious? They want to break the contract with the exporter, and they want to prevent him flooding the market with cheap imitations. But after three years of drought no one has the money for a lawyer. And anyway, they don't know how to get one."

Latif shook his head. "It's not going to be as easy to stop him as you think. I was told of many problems this morning. This one will have to take its place on the list."

"Oh, the men's issues come first, do they?" She sat up straighter, outraged.

"I'll do what I can, Jalia. It just won't happen instantly."

Suddenly she was furious. How dare he care so little for his own people? The women had talked to her about their concerns till her head was ringing, and she had been so sure of his interest!

"I suppose there's no point telling you about all the plans and ideas those women and I talked over? With your head so full of priority masculine stuff?"

"I am sure they asked you to pass such things on to me, thinking as they did that you had agreed to be my wife."

She ignored the thread of steely anger. "They did. But then, they thought you were *their* Shahin as well as their husbands'."

"No, that is not what they think. What they think is that I love you and that I will give my wife anything she asks. That is why they appealed to you."

"But they were wrong," she suggested.

His eyes flicked away from the perilous road for one burning moment. "They were right. But you are not my wife. Ask me as my wife and I will do what you ask."

"That's outrageous!" she snapped. "Why don't you do it for them? They are your people!"

"They are your people, too, Jalia. All Bagestanis are your people. And what are you doing for them? Do not preach to me, when you yourself will turn your back on me and on your country to live abroad as soon as we return!"

"Are you going to punish the Marzuqi women because I won't do what you want?"

"Look at it another way. You have the power to help these women by marrying me."

Electricity shivered her skin as his hand left the wheel and he clasped the back of her head, turning her to face him.

"Marry me, Jalia!" he said urgently. "Don't you see it? You are my woman. My home calls to you, my people touch your heart! This tells you something, if you are listening."

She broke from his hold and turned away.

"Answer me!"

"I've already answered you, Latif. I'm English, for God's sake! I can't do it."

The road hung over a precipice so sheer and stony her heart leaped into her mouth.

"Can't? What does that mean—can't?" he demanded, as a magnificent panorama opened out before them. The road now passed through a three-sided cavity in the side of the mountain. The fourth side was open onto vastness.

"Do you really expect someone born and raised in a city like London to be able to make this kind of transition? I can't just take up a completely new way of life! I'd go mad after a month!"

Far, far below, a ribbon of river wound its way along a rugged chasm of green trees and rust-red rock.

Jalia gasped hoarsely. She'd never seen anything so powerfully moving as this country, with its alternating rugged mountains and green valleys. But this vista staggered her with its lonely magnificence.

"You can!" he growled.

"My whole life is elsewhere, Latif."

"Don't talk like a Westerner who understands nothing but money. Your heart is here—how can your life be elsewhere?"

"My God, will you watch the road? Do you know how steep this drop is?"

"I know this road as I know your heart—better than you do yourself."

"I know my *mind* extremely well. That is what counts."

"Do not be such a fool."

"What's your definition of fool? A woman who disagrees with you?"

Two angry emeralds blazed wrath at her.

"Last night you learned that you love me. Why can you not hold to this? It is weakness, what you do now!"

"Last night we made love, Latif. That's all. Wonderful as it was, and I'm not denying that—"

"You insult me. Am I a technician, to be complimented so?"

"Oh, there's no pleasing you!" she snapped.

"But yes, I am easy to please. You know the way."

Thirteen

After the night in the valley, the relationship between her and Latif grew progressively more edgy. Their exchanges were barbed, and neither seemed able to say anything that didn't have a double meaning.

At night, though everything in him said he was digging his grave deeper with every moment they spent in loving, he could not resist her. However harsh their daily conversation, however determined he became not to succumb this time, when night fell in the tent and her soft breathing filled the silence, his voice called to her of its own accord, and his hands, driven by unbearable hunger, reached for her, found her.

And for Jalia it was the same. Whatever he said in the day to anger or upset her, however resentful her heart when she climbed into her sleeping bag, at the first touch of Latif's hands all resistance melted, and she turned into his embrace with a sigh of need that always blasted the last of his control.

His lovemaking was fierce but tender, as if he never forgot that he was making love to his wife, the mother of his children. The deep respect, the reverence, almost, in his body's embrace meant that her whole being opened to him, and the trusting openness drove his passion to the wildest heights.

Then he called to her soul with terms of endearment he had never before used to any woman. Then he was like a man who has inherited a most precious jewel—touching it, stroking it, admiring its unmatchable beauty, and always his heart breaking a little with the knowledge that it could never be truly his own.

During the days, he punished her for that, for the way her beauty of soul and face and body remained remote and unattainable, for the fact that however deep his own knowledge that their love was the destiny of both of them, she could withhold a part of herself even in the depths of loving.

"You love me," he would accuse her, as his body moved in hers, provoking her to a throaty song of gratitude. And *yes,* she would reply.

"You are mine—say it, Jalia! Tell me you are mine forever!" *Latif, please don't ask me that,* she would say, driving him to a frenzy of passionate lovemaking, his body certain that the way to break down this last resistance was through pleasure that maddened her.

Sometimes his body was right. Sometimes he heard her say, *yes, Latif, yes, whatever you want, oh, God, I've never felt anything like this....*

Later, when the pleasure had faded, she always reneged. Then she would blame him for trying to hold her to promises extracted under duress.

"Duress?" he had rasped the first time she used the word. *"Duress?"*

"The duress of pleasure," she said unapologetically. He laughed angrily, but she stuck to her guns. "It's not fair to ask me to change my mind when I'm actually out of my mind. Of course I'll say anything you want to hear, when I'm effectively drunk with sex.

"I've never felt before what I feel with you. I have no defences. So whatever you make me say in the heat of the moment, Latif, I reserve the right to retract it when I'm sane and sober again."

Of course he was torn—between the satisfaction of knowing he gave her such unequalled pleasure, and the grief of that pleasure not carrying the conviction for her that it did for him, that through it they were united for all time.

Nowhere during the long journey did they hear news of a plane in trouble during the last big storm.

As they proceeded the task became really thankless, for as the mountains got steeper and more rugged, Jalia could no longer see very far from the road. They might be missing a wreckage that was only yards away behind a ridge or an outcrop.

And they could explore only so far on foot. The binoculars were virtually useless now, and though she still carried them around her neck, there was rarely any point in raising them to her eyes.

"When we reach Matar Filkoh airport, we'll turn around and start back," Jalia heard Latif say one day.

"There is no real reason even to continue to the airport—if the plane had passed anywhere close, they'd have picked it up on radar. But we need to radio for news."

Jalia heaved a sigh, and felt tears threaten. She knew in her heart Latif was right. They had covered all the territory they could by road. Either the plane had gone down in an area so remote that only search planes or climbers could hope to find it, or Noor and Bari hadn't flown this way.

And she couldn't be more glad to get out of this truck and away from Latif Abd al Razzaq Shahin if he were a real falcon daily tearing at the liver of her resolve. And yet...

"No!" she protested.

A wave of doubt and denial washed over her. What if the plane's wreckage was just one crag further on? It wasn't stretching hope too far that Noor and Bari could have survived a crash, might be waiting just beyond the next rise, praying for rescue.

Latif turned an emerald-chip gaze her way. "What are you saying?" he asked disbelievingly.

"We can't just give up!"

His jaw tightened, and she understood how much he wanted this to be over. Well, whose fault was it that they couldn't stand being in close confines together? Who had started the trouble?

"The road ends at the airport. After that it is little better than a trail leading to Joharistan."

Joharistan was the tiny country whose name was practically synonymous with remote inaccessibility and tribal unrest.

But Jalia had become too guilt ridden, too sharply

aware of how much her own stupidity must be to blame for Noor's flight. She couldn't give up till the last ditch. Her heart quailed at the thought of having to face her family without having some news to give them.

And if staying longer with Latif was her penance—well, it was a just one, wasn't it?

"There must be something more we can do," she said.

"Do you mean go on foot? What a futile exercise that would be."

Latif waved his hand at the mountains beyond the windscreen. "Where would you go? What direction? You might only succeed in getting hurt yourself, and provoking another air search."

Jalia gazed out the window at the rugged rock face above, and knew defeat.

"There must be something we can do!" she protested anyway.

"Not here."

"I don't believe you! You don't like being with me. You want out of the situation, that's all it is!"

Latif slammed on the brakes and turned to her, showing his teeth.

"Of course I want out of it!" he shouted, as if goaded past his self-control at last. "Do you think I like the torment—every night believing that I have convinced you, and every morning learning that you are a woman who can be confused by my lovemaking, but never convinced by my love? Knowing all the day long that I will not be able to resist the compulsion to try again, learning to half accept that all I will have in the end is the memory of what one day you will remember as a wild affair, and I as the crossroads of my life? Of course I want out!

"You are my future, one way or the other, Jalia— either as the memory of what I could not make mine, or as my wife and the mother of my children. Do you think I don't know that the longer I am with you now, not resisting what I should resist, the harder the memory of the loss will be? Do you think it makes me happy to feed on scraps, constantly hoping for a meal, knowing that after this, any other food will be tasteless to me?"

She gasped under the assault, while feeling charged through her like hot tears in her blood. Without another word he turned and put the vehicle in gear.

"I'm sorry," she faltered. "I didn't—"

He gestured once with an angry hand. "Do not tell me you—"

The truck's wheels slid dangerously into the massive rain-ruts he had been avoiding, and in the next instant he was totally absorbed with preventing the truck from sliding backwards into a gully.

Jalia watched his hands on the wheel, hard and expert, and felt a thrill of remembered delight. Just so did he guide her body when it was at the edge of an abyss of soaring pleasure.

For a crazy moment she wished that he would stop struggling and let them go over the edge now, and relieve her of the daily torture of not knowing her own mind. Sometimes it did seem to her that only death would resolve the dilemma in her heart.

It was tearing her in two. At night, in his arms, she was secure in the conviction his loving closeness induced in her—that love could conquer all. Then she was filled with a divine certainty that her true future lay not in England, but here in the land of her forebears, side by side with this strong, loving man, struggling to make a new life for herself and him and the country.

In the bright light of morning, all the opposing certainty came rushing back, and she called herself a fool for imagining that she could forget all her life to date, make a new self of herself, pretend she belonged in this rugged land.

Then she felt he cheated, took advantage of her sexual susceptibility, gave her the wild pleasure she experienced in his arms only as the means to an end.

And yet, now that he was offering to end the ordeal, she had refused. Did that mean she secretly wanted this torment to go on?

Jalia wasn't at all used to second-guessing herself like this; it made her uncomfortable in her own skin. Until now she had always felt a measure of certainty over her choices, a certainty that was unassailable.

Or, perhaps, had never been deeply challenged. When she had made up her mind to reject her parents' life map, they had given in with sadness but little argument.

When she had made her life-directing decisions—to be an academic, for example—life had given in without much fuss. She hadn't found a position at the prestigious university of her choice, but she had been hired at a small, reputable university, a post that could easily lead to the greater things she still envisioned.

Life hadn't ever really fought back. Now that it was doing so, Jalia made the discovery that self-doubt is an enemy so potent and crippling no other may be necessary.

So for a moment now, watching with fascinated detachment as Latif brought the truck under control, she didn't reject the thought of oblivion as an end to her disquiet.

Or perhaps it was just that she was now dealing with almost unbearable guilt—the guilt of having tried so hard to convince Noor that she was making a dangerous, foolhardy leap in marrying Bari al Khalid. As long as she was here, searching, she didn't have to face what perhaps they had faced days ago at home—that hope diminished with every passing day.

If she had recognized what was really frightening her, if she had faced her own dangerous weakness relative to Latif instead of transferring it...Noor might never have had the second thoughts that had caused her flight.

"There is another road from Matar Filkoh that leads down to the plain and takes a different route back to al Bostan. It is not a good road, but I will ask at the airport if it is still passable after the rains. If it is, we can return that way. But it is futile to talk of going further into the mountains."

Jalia nodded, not trusting herself to speak. Never had she been so filled with guilt and self-doubt. Never had she been so unsure of her course.

They radioed home from the airport, but learned nothing new. The air search hadn't yet been abandoned, but only because of who was missing. For less high profile people, the search would have been given up long ago. Latif and Jalia reported their own lack of success, and both sides were more depressed after the call than before.

The road down was terrifyingly rugged, with the truck bouncing and jolting and threatening to pitch over the edge every five miles.

If she had had to drive it herself, Jalia would have turned tail (if there had been any room to do so) and fled back up to Matar Filkoh and the other road home.

Worse, the terrain made it impossible to pitch the tent, or even to find a comfortable spot for a sleeping bag. They spent their nights cramped and uncomfortable in the truck, while a wolfish wind howled around outside, battering their tiny haven and screeching into every crevice.

Jalia, lying on the back seat while Latif slept half-sitting in the front passenger seat, listened to the wind for hours in the night, where guilt and doubt took renewed strength from the darkness.

Each night she wrestled with the urgent need to sit up, bend over Latif, kiss him awake, and beg him to comfort her, to love her, to decide her terrible dilemma for her.

It was a massive relief when they finally found themselves back on the plain, with brown and gold and green stretching flat for miles ahead. And how glad she was to see villages again, and discover that for other people, ordinary life had gone on during her ordeal.

Still they got no news of Bari's plane.

Every day was making it more likely that the plane had headed out over the sea, for in not one village anywhere did Jalia and Latif find anyone who had heard or seen any sign of a distressed plane on the day of the storm.

"If they did come down over water…" Jalia began hesitantly, when at yet another village they had drawn a blank. She broke off, and Latif glanced at her.

"There is no way to say. It depends on how they came down. If they were hit by lightning, or they broke up in the air, then it is as God wills. But if Bari was able to bring it down with some kind of control—there is a life raft aboard the plane."

"But then why wouldn't they have activated the plane's EPIRB?" she pointed out sadly. "Or at least set off some flares."

The signalling device from Bari's plane, which would have allowed survivors to be found within hours, had never been activated, which was the single biggest argument against the couple's survival. If they had both been so hurt they couldn't find and activate the EPIRB, how long could they have lasted without rescue?

Jalia had begun this search full of hope and the determination that two such vibrant people as Noor and Bari couldn't just die like that, just disappearing into nothing. They would have had to leave some trace.

But as the days stretched into weeks, her hopes had begun to dim. Now she just wanted to get home, to the comfort of the family and familiar surroundings, where perhaps the grieving process had already begun.

They both greeted the approach to Medinat al Bostan with relief.

As they caught sight of the great golden dome of

the mosque and its picturesque minarets glowing in the hot, bright sunshine, Jalia was suddenly sharply aware of how grubby she was, and began to yearn for a long, warm bath, and her comfortable bed, with a power that had never assailed her on the road.

It was just before lunch when they drove between the gates into the great palace that now housed the Sultan again, after thirty years as a museum.

Jalia clambered out of the car, too tired to be anything but grateful when one of the servants who materialized dived for her backpack as she tried to shoulder it.

"Is there any news of the Princess, Massoud?" she asked, and as she expected, the man sighed gloomily.

"Nothing at all, Your Highness. And you—?"

"We found nothing." With Latif close behind, she followed Massoud under the arched passageway into the beautiful private courtyard, where she stood for a moment looking around her.

All around the courtyard arches and columns presented the eye with the comfort of perfection. With a delicious babble the fountain tossed diamonds up to be kissed by sunshine in endlessly repeated beauty; trees waved patterns of shadow against the worn tile over which her ancestors' feet had passed for generations; and ripe pomegranates weighted the branches of the tall shrubs, presenting their rich redness invitingly close.

Jalia reached out to stroke the dimpled fruit with a luxurious sigh. Would she ever get used to such beauty? "*Allah,* it's good to be—"

The look in Latif's green eyes made her suddenly conscious, and she choked the word back.

"Home?" he prompted.

"Jalia!" She heard the urgent voice overhead and looked up to see her mother anxiously leaning over a balcony. "Thank heaven you're back!"

Jalia's heart kicked hard. "Has there been news, Mother?"

"Yes—*no*, not about Noor," her mother cried. She flicked a glance at Latif. "But..."

"For heaven's sake, what is it?" Jalia called anxiously. "Mother, what's happened?"

"Well, darling—Michael rang yesterday."

So far from her thoughts was her previous life that Jalia only blinked. "Michael?"

Princess Muna cleared her throat. "Your fiancé, Jalia. He's flying out today."

"Flying out where?" she asked blankly.

"Here. He's coming..."

Latif's eyes were the precise green of jealous fury. She thought she had never seen anything more coldly beautiful, or more compellingly frightening, in her life.

"*Here?*" she almost shrieked. "Why?"

Her mother's eyebrows went up. "He said something about your hour of need."

"*What?*"

"His flight arrives in two hours," said her mother.

Fourteen

"There is absolutely no reason for you to come with me!"

In dark glasses and with a scarf hiding her hair like a fifties Hollywood starlet, Jalia hissed her continuing protest as she strode into the concourse to wait for Michael's plane. Latif followed as close as her shadow.

"But yes," Latif Abd al Razzaq contradicted calmly.

"You'll only draw attention to us both. People know who you are, Latif. They're bound to start wondering who I am!"

"I wish to meet Michael," he said, with an immovability that made her want to sink her nails into something.

"And why can't you wait to meet him at the pal—

at home? This is ridiculous! All we need is for some damned journalist to be here, casting around…''

''I want to meet your fiancé,'' Latif repeated.

''He is *not* my fiancé,'' she hissed furiously.

''And then I wonder why he has come here.''

''I wonder, too, Latif. But can we get one thing straight? You do not have the right to this little show of jealous possessiveness!'' Her hand flattened the air. ''I made it clear from the outset that—''

''Do you talk about rights? I talk about love. There are no rights and wrongs. There is only—I want to see this man you tell me is not your fiancé. If you have told me the truth about him, why do you fear my meeting him?''

''I do not fear your meeting him!'' she lied fervently, though she didn't know herself why she feared a meeting. Perhaps because she didn't understand Michael's motives in coming here.

The Arrivals doors opened into the small waiting area and in ones and twos the people from the latest flight started trickling out. Jalia licked her lips and nervously began to watch their faces.

''Jalia!'' Michael's voice cried, and she turned to see him break away from a small group just emerging through the door, to stride towards her. He had lost none of the attention-seeking flair that made Michael a star amongst the staid university lecturers.

People turned to look, and Jalia instinctively lifted a hand to adjust her sunglasses and dropped her head.

A moment later Michael grabbed her close for a warm, enthusiastic hug.

''Darling, how good of you to meet me yourself

when you must be nearly exhausted. Desperately sorry I couldn't get here sooner!''

''Hello, Michael. This is a surprise! I—''

His arms still tight around her, he gave her a firm peck on her mouth that effectively silenced her, kissed her on each cheek, and lifted his head to smile a warning down into her startled face.

''I'm surprised, too! I certainly wasn't expecting to see you! Your mother said you were out scouring the mountains! When did you get back?''

She was acutely, uncomfortably aware of Latif standing behind her, watching with unblinking attention and restrained fury, a falcon choosing his moment to strike.

''A couple of hours ago. Michael, why on earth—''

''Not a word now, darling!'' Michael hushed her with another little kiss, and she sensed his discomfort. He really was not happy that she had met him. ''Plenty of time to talk.''

''Yes. Michael, this is Latif Abd al Razzaq,'' she said, easing out of the embrace. ''He—''

Michael didn't go for the dark, hawklike type, and he scarcely looked at Latif. ''Great!'' he said, grabbing his hand. ''Great to meet you! You look after the Princess, I imagine.''

Latif stood unmoving as a rock, so obviously dangerous that Jalia cowered for Michael. But he was oblivious.

''I take good care of her, as you will see,'' Latif murmured.

''Great!'' Michael said again. ''Any news about Noor, darling?''

''No, nothing new. Let's go, Michael. Is that the

only luggage you brought?'' She could see nothing but a leather carry-on bag slung over his shoulder. It looked new and very expensive. Too expensive for an underpaid university lecturer.

"I had no idea what clothes I'd need at the palace," he explained breezily. "For all I knew I might need a *djellaba!*"

"Michael, could you lower your voice, please?" she murmured. "There might be journalists around. Latif—"

Michael's laughter was long, loud and false. "But of course there are journalists around!" He turned and held out a conjuror's hand towards a sharp-faced young blond woman standing nearby.

"Meet Ellin Black—from the *Evening Herald.* You probably know her name. Ellin, my very own Princess Bride!"

"Great to meet you, Princess," said Ellin Black, smiling at her with cool, self-possessed assessment. Her eyes flicked to Latif and widened with such an expression of curiosity, interest and female intent that Jalia would have laughed, except that she didn't feel like laughing. "And who are you?"

"I look after the Princess," Latif said smoothly.

"And John is the *Herald* photographer," said Ellin, quickly disowning any closer relationship with a fair, heavyset, middle-aged man a few feet away.

John Bentinck lifted his hand away from his face and genially nodded at them before fitting the video camera to his eye again.

"Sit down, Michael," Jalia said crisply, leading the way into her private apartment at the palace an hour later. She was absolutely furious, and not hiding it well. "What would you like to drink?"

"I'm absolutely gasping for a cup of tea," he said.

They had driven from the airport in silence, Jalia furious with his betrayal, and Michael almost equally angry because she had refused to let the journalists into the car. At first he had tried to explain how brilliant a coup it had been for him to sign an exclusive with the *Herald*, then had descended into sullen silence.

In the front seat beside the driver Latif might as well have been carved in stone—not that Michael spared a thought for her "bodyguard." But Jalia had been nervous and edgy all the way, wondering when and how he would pounce.

He never did. On their arrival at the palace, he simply bowed and disappeared, leaving Jalia even more anxious, and faintly disappointed.

Of course she would have to sort this out with Michael privately, and yet—it would have been so much easier if Latif had insisted on staking his claim.

Jalia reminded herself that Latif had no claim. She had told him so herself. What had she been expecting? That he would knock Michael down? Send him packing?

Belatedly, very belatedly, she saw that she should have forced the showdown at the airport before Ellin Black got the wrong idea. Michael had found some way to cash in on the situation, that was clear. And it was going to involve publicity. By not denying their engagement instantly, she had given him a credibility that might now be harder to dislodge.

Why hadn't she seen things so clearly an hour ago?

But she had been so obsessed with avoiding notice, with not causing any kind of public scene that might get into the papers, that she had missed the chance to deliver a short, sharp shock.

It was all Latif's fault! If she hadn't been so worried about what he was thinking, she might have dealt with this better. And if only *he* had said something, Michael might have realized...

She brought herself up short. How could she have such ridiculously contradictory thoughts?

In a cool voice Jalia dispatched the ever-attentive servant for tea and fruit juice, then settled in a chair.

Michael stood in the doorway to the balcony under the arched framework of stained glass, gazing out at the courtyard. Across the way the rows of similar arches lay in picturesque light and shade. The music of the fountain and birdsong were the only sounds that met the ear.

"This is fabulous!" he exclaimed after a few minutes of silent appreciation. "Beats the new palaces all to hell, doesn't it? Look at that tiling—I've been on digs where we've found floors just like that dating from eight hundred years ago! The place must be—"

"Yes, Ghasib had some justification for turning the palace into a museum," she agreed. "It's still open to the public, of course, except for this wing, where the family live."

"The family!" Michael said, laughing and shaking his head. "You know, no one was all that surprised. In the Senior Common Room people were joking about how they used to call you the Ice Princess. Did you know that? They were walking around saying, 'Well, we always knew!'"

He laughed, but Jalia didn't. The servant returned with a tray, and when he had set it down she quietly dismissed him.

"No, I never knew it," she said, with a calm she didn't feel. "Come and have your tea."

He left his admiration of the courtyard from another age and sank onto the sofa opposite her as the door closed behind the servant.

Jalia poured out the amber liquid, passed him the small gold-traced crystal cup and said, "What exactly do you hope to get out of this, Michael?"

He laughed a little anxiously. "Come on, Jalia! There's no need to take that tone! You're getting what you want out of the engagement. Why shouldn't I benefit, too?"

"That's what you call it? You've come here without warning, at a hugely difficult moment for me and my entire family, with a sleazy tabloid journalist in tow—"

"Ellin is hardly *sleazy!*" he said. "And how was I to know you'd take it so hard? What's so terrible if our engagement is publicly known? How does it affect your life, Jalia?"

"I think the point is, how does it affect *yours?*"

He carefully chose a lump of sugar, set it between his teeth, and sipped his tea like an expert.

"A huge difference. You would not believe." He leaned forward earnestly, the cup held loosely between his knees, but looked down at it instead of at her.

"Listen, Jalia—you know I've been trying for

years for the chance to examine the private antique art collections of the Princes of the Barakat Emirates—and Ghasib's, too, before the Sultan's return.

"You know what a boost it would be for my academic prospects if I succeeded. And do I have to remind you that these are difficult times in the academic world?"

"No, you don't have to remind me," she said stonily.

Sudden animation lit his features. "Do you remember that Mithra plate forgery Jasmin Shaw published a few years ago, suggesting that the theme had been copied from a genuine original? Do you know there's a rumour making the rounds now that, during the Parvan-Kaljuk War, when he was selling off his treasures, the King of Parvan actually sold King Daud of the Barakat Emirates a Mithra plate? And it's now hidden away in Prince Rafi's private collection? If I could—"

"Michael. What has this got to do with our engagement?"

"Oh, don't be naive," he challenged irritably. "You're related to these families now, Jalia! Engaged to you, I'm not just an ordinary academic anymore, am I? I'm inside the charmed circle."

He paused to drain his cup, and set it down.

"The *Herald* has contracted with me for a regular column discussing the antique treasures of the Gulf of Barakat—but it has to include some never-before-seen pieces from the palace collections.

"It's going to put Middle Eastern antiquities on the map, Jalia, and there's talk about my hosting a television series if it's a success. This represents a huge forward step for my career.''

She stared at him in disbelief. *''Tabloids? Television?* I didn't realize you had ambitions to become a popular art historian.''

Michael, in common with many academics, had always sneered at colleagues who took their wisdom to the *hoi polloi*. Stooping to inform the general public wasn't an occupation for the true scholar. Not even for ready money.

''I didn't realize it myself, till the *Herald* put it to me. But beggars can't be choosers, Jalia. And university budgets are only getting tighter, aren't they?''

Jalia set her glass down with a little *chink.* ''And you thought that a fake engagement with me would open all those doors for you?''

''Why not?''

''Because it is *fake,* Michael. It was wrong of me to lie to my parents like that, though I thought I had good reason. But to go on lying and extend it to the Princes of the Barakat Emirates and Ashraf and everyone else would be worse than wrong. It would be an appalling abuse.''

''It doesn't have to be a lie.'' She saw the shadow of a haunted desperation in his eyes. ''We could get married.''

''What?''

''Just for a short time. What difference would it make to you, Jalia? We could get divorced in a year, say, no hard feelings. We've been good friends, haven't we? This could make me, Jalia. There's such a lot riding on it. More than you know,'' he added unhappily.

She stared at him in appalled silence.

"Michael, do you know what you're saying?" she whispered. "What has put the idea into your head?"

"You did, Jalia."

"But it's out of the question! You must see that it's impossible! I want to end this engagement farce immediately. If you hadn't been on your way here when I got back to al Bostan, I'd have phoned you to tell you so."

"But why, if it's serving your purpose? Jalia, please consider!"

"It's over, Michael. I'm sorry if it now puts you in the embarrassing position of being publicly dumped, but there's no one to blame but yourself for that. We agreed to tell no one but my parents. And in your heart you *know* you shouldn't have done this without checking with me first."

There was a long silence while Michael stared at her, stricken.

"Jalia," he said. "I'm really, really sorry. I really had no idea that you'd react like this. I just didn't know. And I've done something so stupid—it's not going to be as easy as that, I'm afraid."

She gazed at him in mounting anxiety. He was so white he looked sick.

"My God, what is it? What can you possibly have done?"

Michael leaned forward, clearing his throat.

"Ellin took me out after I'd cut the deal with the features editor. To the Savoy. We got into celebrating my new future…Jalia, I've never had so much Moët et Chandon poured down me in my life. I got pissed, and I mean completely pissed."

Premonitory dread shivered her skin. ''Oh, Michael!''

He sat shaking his head, white and desperate. ''She got the truth out of me. I'm sorry, Jalia. When I sobered up I was just—''

''The truth?'' Jalia whispered, but she knew. ''The truth about what?''

''That Princess Jalia was so terrified of being forced into marriage by her parents here in Bagestan that she begged her gay friend to pretend to an engagement.''

''Oh, *God!*''

''Ellin really wants to use it, but because the deal I've cut depends on our engagement being real, she can't. She says that's a story that's really got legs— with Princess Noor missing, you know, and pretty well presumed dead.

''People are already suggesting maybe Noor ran to avoid a forced marriage, and Ellin says the story would really give that rumour weight. 'Imagine how the world would condemn Princess Noor's parents for putting her into the position where she chose death over an unhappy marriage,' she said to me.''

Jalia felt as if all the oxygen had suddenly been sucked from the room.

''So we've got to go on with the engagement, Jalia. I'm sorry, but unless you want the truth blasted all over the front page, we have to go on with it. I'm sorry, love. Sorrier than I can say. You can kick me black and blue if you want, but no blacker than I've already kicked myself.''

Jalia gazed at him, not really focusing on Michael at all. She was thinking how strange it was that she should choose such a moment as this to understand at last that she was in love with Latif Abd al Razzaq.

Fifteen

ENGAGED TO A PRINCESS!

A *Herald* Exclusive

Dr. Michael Wickliffe, 32, collector and Middle Eastern art history lecturer at Scotland's small but prestigious King James VI University, has particular reason to smile. Not only has his marriage proposal been accepted by the beautiful woman he knew only as Jalia Shahbazi, a fellow lecturer at the university, but she's also recently been revealed as a princess! Jalia is a first cousin of Sultan Ashraf al Jawadi, recently crowned in Bagestan....

At one end of the private courtyard an arched terrace caught the early sun, and since Noor's and Bari's disappearance a communal breakfast had been regularly served there.

Newspapers from around the world were on offer with the coffee, and in addition a radio, television and telephones had been set up.

Knowing what the morning papers would say, Jalia had come down early—but, she saw with dismay, not early enough. Latif was sitting alone at the table, an English paper open in front of him.

At the sound of footsteps, he lifted his head from the newsprint. Jalia's steps stopped abruptly as she saw his face, white and cold and harsh as a judge.

"Latif!" she whispered, her voice catching so that she had to stop and cough.

She had hoped to see him first, to try and explain, but last night there had been yet another reported sighting of Noor, this time on a French ferry. It had taken hours to confirm what they all instinctively guessed, that it was false, and she could not get him alone.

He tossed the paper and his table napkin down, every movement measured and deliberate, and stood. His chair squealed a protest against the tiles.

"So you did not deny your fiancé's story."

"No, because—I mean, he's not..."

His emerald eyes narrowed with ferocious feeling. "He is not your fiancé?"

His voice was terrible, raw and harsh and angrily contemptuous. Jalia flinched. "Well..."

"The journalist has printed a lie?"

She began to stammer. "Yes. Well, not exactly, but—"

She swallowed and pressed her lips together. She

did not know him. He was an angry, frightening stranger now, his fury lashing around her.

"Make up your mind," he said, and she had never heard such coldness in Latif's voice before.

"We have to go on pretending for the moment," she said in a gulp, and under his fierce gaze she stammered out the explanation.

Latif stood looking down at her, his face as unmoved and unmoving as rock, and she realized even before he said it that she was too late. Her understanding had come too late. Her love was too late.

"You use the engagement now as you used it before—to make yourself safe from me," he rasped. "But you no longer need this fiction. You are safe from me, Jalia."

"No! Why won't you believe me? It's the truth!"

He shrugged. "It is the truth, then. And what do you want now?"

Her heart beat with dread. She hadn't guessed it would be so hard, that she would have to spell it all out. She hadn't allowed herself to imagine that when she finally told her love Latif would no longer be interested.

"Nothing," she faltered. "I just wanted you to know how it had happened."

"Why?"

"Perhaps you've forgotten you once declared an interest in the matter. You said you loved me."

She lifted her head and forced herself to meet his eyes.

"Well, I love you, too, Latif. I'm sorry I found out so late, but I have found out. I love you, and I—I

want to be with you, and if that means coming to
Bagestan..."

His emerald gaze fixed hers, and for a moment her
heart beat with hope so powerful she was almost suf-
focated.

"You will move to Bagestan for my sake?"

"Yes, if that's what you want. Yes."

"Jalia, you speak to me as the fiancée of another
man," he said coldly. "Are you not ashamed of such
betrayal?"

"I told you, this is being forced on me! I told you
what the journalist told Michael...."

"And why did you not come to me before letting
this story be printed?"

"What could you have done?"

His eyes narrowed suddenly, so that she gave an
involuntary little gasp.

"That is no longer important. Now you have admitted to the engagement, and refuse to deny it. What
do you expect me to do now?"

"Nothing! I'm waiting for things to sort themselves
out with Noor and Bari first, and we'll find a way to
get out of the engagement without a fuss."

"It is as I said. He wants to marry you. Doesn't he?"

She shifted uncomfortably. "Not really."

He stared at her from unreadable eyes.

She swallowed. "It's not what you think." Everything was backwards and upside down—how could
she explain that Michael's reasons for wanting to
marry her were so unlike Latif's? "We'll announce
that the engagement's over as soon as—"

"And what shall I do in the meantime?" he demanded contemptuously. "Watch you as the prom-

ised wife of another man, and smile, and wait my turn? Or shall we cheat your fiancé as before?''

"Latif, I love you!" How could it all go so wrong? Why couldn't she explain? Why couldn't he understand?

"A weak love, Jalia, if you can be happy to be engaged to someone else."

"It isn't like that!"

She flung herself against him, her arms reaching around his neck, her face pressing against his throat, her tears hot and wet on her lashes, sobs shaking her. But he stood unresponsive under the embrace, until, utterly shamed, she released him and stood back.

"No, Jalia. I have had enough of humiliation and lies. I have learned my lesson. Now you learn yours."

His face then she would never forget, not if she made a hundred.

ALL THAT GLITTERS...

And while we're on the subject of the al Jawadi—is the recently announced engagement of Princess Jalia and Dr. Michael Wickliffe all it appears? It seems that on her first visit to Bagestan, the woman they call the Ice Princess melted in a big way for one of the Sultan's handsome Cup Companions. Yet as soon as she returned to the U.K., she and Wickliffe privately announced their engagement. According to close friends, the move was a big surprise. Is there something the beaming fiancé should know?

"I hope you'll consider taking a position in one of the universities here," the Sultana was saying to Michael. "Under Ghasib, of course, the universities suffered from chronic poor funding—he knew good universities would be a source of dissent. Everyone who could studied abroad. But I'm sure you know Ash is very determined to improve the standards."

On Friday nights, the Sultan and Sultana hosted a family dinner, either in their private apartments or in the private courtyard of the palace. Members of the family and Cup Companions had a standing invitation.

Tonight the traditional *sofreh* was spread on the grass by the tumbling fountain. The first such gathering Jalia had attended had been soon after she and her family arrived in Bagestan, and then her heart had thrilled to the sight of her restored family, so numerous, sitting and lying on the grass while they put away vast quantities of perfectly cooked rice and lamb, bean stew, chicken with pomegranate sauce, and bowlfuls of pomegranate seeds so red and delicious she had felt she was eating rubies.

Tonight she wasn't enjoying herself. Not with Michael here, being welcomed and treated as her fiancé—for they were all in enough grief and turmoil over Noor without Jalia giving everyone more cause for concern.

"Thank you, Sultana. It's an option we'll certainly consider," Michael said, preening a little under the implied flattery, then went for broke. "I wonder if anything is planned about cataloguing the remains of the old royal collections? I might be very helpful there."

Jalia had told the Sultana the truth, just a few

minutes ago, when at Dana's suggestion the two women had gone walking together in the garden. It was clear the Sultana had sensed something, and even though the timing couldn't have been worse, Jalia had submitted to temptation.

"I think you're making the right choice," Dana had said, after hearing her out. "The engagement's public now—there's nothing to be gained from rushing headlong into breaking it. Your image wouldn't be improved by the move, and we can definitely do without another media feeding frenzy right now."

Jalia sighed. It had been a huge relief to confide in the Sultana. And an even bigger one to know the Sultana didn't think she was *too* much of a fool.

"That being said, however, we have to find a way out of this as soon as possible. I don't know how the gossip about the engagement got going, but it puts you in a very awkward position," the Sultana had murmured, her eyes wandering towards where Latif sat on the grass. "But we have to talk more another time. Let's get back, or God knows the next story will be about how concerned the Sultana is over the rumours. Not that I think the staff is suspect, but who *is* leaking the rumours?"

Now the Sultana was drawing Michael out, like anyone taking the trouble to get to know her cousin's new fiancé. Latif was sitting at the other end of the spread cloth, an irresistible magnet. Jalia couldn't stop her gaze unconsciously gluing to him.

And as if aware of it, his gaze rose and met hers. Jalia's heart leaped into her eyes. Then she gasped and drew back, like someone who has been unexpectedly stung.

His expression was totally indifferent. There was in his gaze no memory of anything between them, no desire, no condemnation, no interest. He didn't even seem to notice that she was a living creature. His glance wandered past, leaving her chilled and shaken.

Oh, how different from that first evening, when the brilliant emerald gaze had been a physical touch on her skin, potent, full of promise and intent. Then it had unnerved her, then she had felt anxious and unsettled, and under threat—not least from her own unrecognized feelings.

Well, Latif's passionate love had had all the staying power of cigarette smoke, and now it was safe to discover what her own real feelings were. Now that she no longer had it, she could admit that his passionate wooing, his approval, the hot possessiveness of his glance had felt like everything she needed to live.

Of course she would never marry Michael, and she had been doubly grateful to hear Dana say the engagement had to be ended soon. But now she saw what filled her with grief—that, whenever that happened, there would be no rekindling Latif's interest.

It was best this way. If she could not resist him— and Jalia was becoming daily more aware how deeply she had been fooling herself about her ability to do that—then thank God he had been made to resist her. She had almost started to believe she could make a go of things in this country.

"I suppose the cataloguing will have to be done sooner or later," Dana was saying, and Jalia came to with no idea of how long she had been in her trance. "But I doubt if it's high on Ash's list of priorities."

"It should be," Michael said, smiling. "The ancient history of Bagestan is enshrined in such treasures, after all. Sultan Hafzuddin's private collection was legendary. It's terribly important to learn what has survived Ghasib's depredations, don't you think?"

The Sultana smiled. "Not quite as important as reestablishing the damaged irrigation system in the villages which had the bad luck to get on the wrong side of Ghasib's agents, I'm sure you'll agree."

"But I wouldn't be of any use there," Michael pointed out with a winning smile.

The Sultana inclined her head.

"No, I see that," she said. Her eyes flicked to Jalia. "I do see."

"Princess!" Latif said, and in her sleep she whimpered his name and instinctively reached for him. "Princess! Wake up!"

The voice was urgent. Jalia came suddenly awake, sitting up almost before her eyes were open. Her bedside lamp threw a soft glow into the shadows. Outside, the first rays of sunrise were lighting the sky.

In the first sleepy moment she could think of only one reason for him to come to her like this.

"Latif!" she sobbed with tearing relief, and reached for him again.

"There's news," he said harshly, stepping back.

She saw that he was dressed, in jeans and a shirt and thin bomber jacket, and she snapped alert. Her heart pounded, closing her throat.

"Is it Noor? What have they found? Is she alive? Is Bari?"

His eyes ran over her as if involuntarily, making her sharply aware of her sleep-ruffled hair, her bare limbs, how incompletely the silk night-slip covered her breasts.

It was only a moment's weakness. He brought his gaze back to her wide-stretched eyes, her white face.

"The EPIRB of Bari's plane has suddenly started sending a signal," he said. "From the area of the Gulf Islands."

"Oh, *alhamdolillah!*" she cried, bursting into tears. "The islands! Oh, Latif, does it mean—they're alive?"

"I hope so, Princess. But we can know nothing till we get to the scene. Two helicopters have been scrambled. Ashraf has asked me to go. Please tell—"

She tossed back the coverlet and slipped to her feet.

"I'm coming with you."

"No," he said. "Ash asks that you help break the news to Noor's parents and your own. Dana will meet you in her sitting room in a few minutes."

Jalia grabbed his arm. "Dana can do it without me. It'll only take me two seconds to put some clothes on. Wait for me. I want—"

Latif's jaw tightened, his eyes flashed. "You are not coming with me! Don't be such a fool! It is no place for you!"

"If Noor is hurt—"

"We will have medics aboard. Do you think the Sultan is a fool?"

She put out a pleading hand. "Latif—"

He caught her wrist in a hold that hurt. "Do you listen to nothing and no one? Go and—"

But it had been a mistake to touch her. He dragged

her closer and his other hand, of its own volition, buried itself in her tousled hair. Jalia melted against him with a yearning cry that scorched his blood, and his mouth clamped hers.

Hunger and need flooded her, but even as her arm reached up around his neck he dragged it down again, and stepped back. For one long moment they stared at each other, chests heaving, sharply aware of the bed behind her in the golden, inviting lampglow.

The indifference of the past few days had been stripped from him like the mask it was, and her heart was bursting at what she saw in his eyes.

But only for a moment, and then he was back in control.

''Wake her parents. I will be in contact as soon as we have learned anything.''

Sixteen

It always seemed strange to Jalia afterwards that it should be in that anxious hour when the family clung together, pacing and praying, waiting for the news, that she should have understood so much at last. About herself and life. About family and blood and tradition and duty.

About love.

Noor might be alive, she might be dead, or terribly wounded, and whichever it was, she, Jalia, could do nothing to change her cousin's fate.

Life was short and so precious, and was she going to live hers without love? Was she going to run from the challenge life was offering her—the challenge to do some real good in the world? The challenge to love and be loved from the most passionate depths of her soul, and another's?

She had two countries—the land of her birth, and the land of her ancestors, her blood. Each called to her, but only one really needed her. Needed everything that she was and would be. Needed her heart, her mind, her love, her education, her commitment, the life she would live, the children she would have.

In return it offered her its rich history, its beauty, a deep sense of blood connection and belonging, and the heart of a strong, noble lover, a one-of-a-kind man—if she could win him back.

Even if she could not, her future would be in this land, where everything she was and could be would be needed for as long as she cared to give it. Where her contribution would be unique, where her people needed her. Whether he loved her or not…her home was here.

She had seen the truth in Latif's eyes—he did love her. His indifference had been a disguise. But that didn't mean she could make him change his mind.

Their prayers were answered as the sun climbed brilliantly into the blue sky, when Latif phoned with the news that Noor and Bari were alive and well.

They had come down in the storm near one of the smallest of the Gulf Islands and had been marooned there the whole time.

Crooning and wailing with joy, Princess Zaynab spoke to her daughter first, and then it was the turn of each of them, father, cousins, aunts, uncles. Jalia was nearly dissolved in the flooding tears that poured out of her eyes as she took her turn and spoke to her cousin and childhood friend.

"Alhamdolillah rabilalamin!" Noor's father began

when they hung up, and the family softly, gratefully, slipped into the recital. *"Al rahman, al raheem."* Praise be to God, the Lord of the World, the Compassionate, the Merciful...

Miracles do happen, however unfashionable it may be in some quarters to think so.

"Please stop punishing yourself," Noor advised gently. "For a start, when I bolted it had nothing to do with anything you said. And anyway, as it turned out, it could be the best thing that's ever happened to me."

Noor had stepped off the helicopter a stranger— thin, bony, her hair a sun-bleached mess, her skin burned and rough...and with an expression in her eyes Jalia had never seen there before.

Jalia burst into overwrought tears. These days she couldn't seem to get any kind of handle on her emotions. "I'm sorry, but it was so awful!" she wept. "Not knowing anything about why you'd gone, where you were. Everyone was secretly blaming me, but not as much as I blamed myself. It was so wrong of me—"

"Wrong?" Noor protested. "You couldn't have been more right! Bari doesn't love me. He never did."

"Oh, Noor," Jalia objected sadly.

Noor lifted her hand from the bathwater, and absently studied her ravaged nails. She had eaten an enormous meal and then slept the clock around. After that the first thing she'd opted for was a bath. The cousins had drained and refilled the tub twice as Noor soaked out the accumulated grime of the island.

"Funny, isn't it, all that newspaper gossip about a forced marriage?" Noor said. "It *was* a forced marriage, but the other way around. I wonder why the media don't get hot and bothered when *men* are the ones being dragged down the aisle as a sacrifice on the altar of family duty?"

"I think Bari is in love with you. He told me…"

"I don't care what he told you."

"He says he should have realized before how he felt, and he fell truly in love with you on the island."

"Really!" Noor said brightly. "Well, he had a funny way of showing it!"

"Noor, can't you just talk to him?"

"And actually, I don't care when he fell in love with me, if he did. He woke up too late. If he did."

"I guess that's how Latif feels about me," Jalia said. "That I woke up too late."

"Oh, Jay!" Noor exclaimed remorsefully, reaching a damp hand out to her. "Oh, what a mess it's all turned out to be, this princess business!"

"Yes, in some ways."

Jalia picked up the little rag doll Noor had brought back with her from the island and absently wiggled its arms. It smelled of smoke and mildew, and a child's distress.

"But not a complete mess." Jalia paused. "Some things are much clearer than they were. I can see my way now, which I never could before. I've lost a big blind spot about Bagestan. I know how much I love this country now. I know I do belong here in spite of everything. I'm going to dig in and help…people like the women of the Sey-Shahin tribe, for example. They're really at a disadvantage trying to deal with the West. They need help. That's really important to me now. And I guess I've got Latif to thank for that, whatever happens.''

She held out the doll, and touched a finger to the pearl necklace around its neck.

"In some refugee camp somewhere in the world, the child who owned this doll is...suffering who knows what torments. I want to do something about that. And I guess that'll have to be enough for me for now.''

She was perilously near tears again.

Noor's eyes were bright.

"Latif loves you, you know. He still loves you. I was watching last night at dinner, and if you could have seen his face, Jalia!''

"Maybe. I don't think he cares whether he loves me or not. I think he's made up his mind that I'm not worth it. That's the problem I'm facing—that he can love me but still not want anything to do with me.''

"You have absolutely got to get out of this engagement thing with Michael!'' Noor said urgently, standing up and beginning to rinse under the shower. "We've got to find a way. Maybe you should just bite the bullet, Jay.''

"Now's not the right time. Not with my parents back in England—they'd get mobbed if the *Herald* ran that story without warning now.''

Noor reached for the fluffy towelling robe and wrapped herself in it with a bone-deep appreciation of its soft luxury that was completely different from the take-it-for-granted attitude Jalia remembered.

"Well, from a purely selfish point of view it's sure easier not having to deal with stories about my supposed forced marriage in addition to everything that's going on now, Jalia, but don't you think our rescue gives you the perfect opportunity to bury the news?''

"I don't think I could stand the media attention right now. Those little smears about Michael and me and the mysterious sheikh I'm after are awful enough without that added. Thank God no one's managed to get Latif's name! That would just kill me! If I ever find out who—'' She broke off, because Noor stared at her, her hand to her mouth.

"Jalia, haven't you seen it?''

"Oh, *no!* What now?''

"On the table in the other room. The *Blatt.*''

Jalia leaped up and ran to the table, scrabbling through the newspapers lying there. Each one had photos of the rescued couple getting out of the helicopter, and happy headlines.

"It's that gossip-column thing opposite the op ed page,'' Noor told her as she came back into the bathroom. "There.''

A water-shrivelled fingertip pointed to a small news item of the kind Jalia had come to dread.

The Gadfly can now reveal the name of the mysteriously impervious Cup Companion who's apparently captured Princess Jalia's heart: it's the dashing Latif Abd al Razzaq Shahin, chief of the Sey-Shahin tribe.

His title, *Shahin,* can be translated as *royal falcon,* and there *is* a certain bird-of-prey air about the Princess's reputed heartthrob.

A source very close to the palace has revealed that the Cup Companion and the Princess were alone together in the mountains, searching for her cousin, Princess Noor, and his friend, Bari al Khalid, throughout the time the couple were missing. A romantic opportunity, you might think, but whatever happened between them, it doesn't seem to have altered the Princess's status.

Nor did it arouse obvious jealous feeling in the heart of Jalia's supposed fiancé, fellow professor Dr. Michael Wickliffe. Could it be that his real love is the antique silver plate in the Sultan's private collection?

"Who did this?" Jalia wailed. "Who told them?" She closed her eyes to squeeze back the hot, bursting tears. "If they start asking me about Latif I'll go mad. Do you think it was Latif who told them? Is it his revenge, making a fool of me, proving something?"

"No, oh no!" Noor protested, shocked. "Oh, honey, I had no idea it would hit you so hard! I'm sorry I told you like that!"

Jalia sobbed, and Noor comforted her and began to weep, too, so that in the end they comforted each other. They both felt better for it.

"You've really changed, too, you know that?" Noor said, as they sat out on the balcony watching the fountain, drinking delicious juice. "You never used to talk about your feelings at all."

"Oh, I absorbed the English virtue of self-control, and like all converts, I took it to extremes," Jalia said with a watery smile.

"And maybe I was never really interested," Noor admitted softly. "Too self-centred, as Bari said."

"Did he say that? That's pretty hard. I guess you can get pretty close to the bone in a situation like that, face-to-face with the struggle to survive."

"When one of you is intent on breaking the other into little pieces, you get very close to the bone, yes," Noor said, with quiet bitterness.

"He didn't break you, though. Maybe he…"

"What?" Noor demanded.

"Well, cut you—like a diamond or something. So that your real self would be revealed."

"Thanks," Noor replied, with a snort of laughter that threatened to turn into a sob. "It was a bloody uncomfortable operation, let me tell you. And come to think of it, I could say the same of you. Latif cut you, but not like a diamond, like a person. Now I can see you bleed."

"It was a bloody uncomfortable operation, let me tell you," Jalia repeated.

The two cousins laughed together, ignoring the tears burning the cheeks of them both.

Seventeen

Creeping along a magical moonlit hallway that belonged to another age, Jalia wondered if she was merely following the trail blazed by her ancestresses in centuries gone by.

Because whoever had designed this wing of the palace had certainly not been unaware of the needs of midnight ramblers—the number of human-sized niches available for ducking into was testament to that. Not that she'd ever noticed that fact until she slipped into one to avoid a passing servant.

The only problem was that most of the niches were home to antique lamps or brass trays or ancient flintlock rifles, their silver mountings decorated with ruby and emerald.

In the past, had it meant death to a woman if she tripped over one and brought the guards?

Her ancestors. Maybe this was simply in her blood—the urge that had suddenly overwhelmed her in the dead of another sleepless night to find her lover's door....

Except that he was not her lover anymore. From the day Michael had arrived, her nights had been filled with loneliness and heartache instead of Latif Abd al Razzaq.

How desperate love could make a person! Jalia thought back to those distant days when she had accused her cousin of falling for Bari based on sexual attraction alone, as if that were nothing much.

Well, she had learned.

She counted the doors again. Oh, let the count be the same on the inside as it was from the balcony side! One broom cupboard would throw her calculations adrift, and how unbelievably embarrassing if she ended up in some other Cup Companion's bed....

Her faint shadow on the moonlit floor wavered and darkened, and she frowned for a moment before she understood. Then with a stifled cry she whirled, to find one of the palace servants in an open doorway behind her.

"Good evening, my Lady," he whispered, showing no surprise. His voice sounded oddly familiar, though she could not recall ever having seen his face before.

"Good evening," Jalia said, and stood gazing blankly at him, unable to come up with any comment that would cover her presence in this corridor at this hour of the night.

Smiling, the man moved past her to a carved wooden door. "Allow me, my Lady," he murmured, opening it softly, and stood waiting for her to enter.

My Lady! Suddenly the strange title registered, and she realized why his voice was familiar—it was the accent she had heard in Sey-Shahin Valley. This man must be one of Latif's personal servants. And what was more, he wouldn't be calling her My Lady unless he had heard about that wedding night in the mountains....

Fire burned in her cheeks, but in the mountain custom he was not looking into her face. Jalia stood for a moment of dreadful, gnawing immobility.

Then she thought of her ancestresses and the niches so artfully created for them and their lovers by the palace architect. Clearly some would have risked death to be with someone they loved. Was she, who had so much less to lose, going to give up because she'd received encouragement?

"Thank you," she whispered, and stepped into the room. He closed the door softly behind her.

She was in a small anteroom lighted only by the moonlight filtering through from another door ahead. She could feel the faint breeze that said the door to the balcony was also open.

A moment later she was standing beside the bed, listening to Latif's deep breathing.

The black moonshadow of a tree in the courtyard danced in the pale blue-white light that played over the balcony, the tiled floor, the silk carpet, the beautifully carved fireplace...Latif's bed.

That was spread on the floor, in the Eastern way, a thick mattress strewn with pillows and cushions and covered with a coverlet like a miniature painting, blue and purple all shot with glittering gold.

The object of her desire lay on his side, one muscled arm outflung as if to wrap someone in against his chest, his hand grasping the pillow. His cheekbone was sharply shadowed, as were his eyes. His mouth was carved as beautifully as a marble statue, his jaw resolute even in sleep.

Jalia's heart was beating in panicked little picket-fence ripples.

Slowly, where she stood, she slipped the thin dressing gown off her shoulders and let it fall to the floor. Underneath she wore the silk pyjamas she had been wearing on their ''wedding'' night in the valley. In the moonlight the pale jade was the colour of smoke.

Barefoot on the sensuously soft carpet, she crept forward to the edge of the bed. Her shadow came between the moon and his face for only an instant before she dropped to her knees, but as if it had been a touch, he stirred.

''Jalia?'' he murmured, in a voice of agonized longing, and her heart kicked so hard the blow would have felled her if she had not already been down.

''Yes,'' she whispered on a sob. ''Yes.''

''What the devil are you doing here?''

She gasped with the shock of the changed tone. Latif sat up, wide awake and furious. The coverlet sliding down his naked chest, he shot one hand out to the lamp on the floor beside the bed.

For a moment they blinked at each other in its glow, his arm still extended to the lamp, frozen in an uncomprehending tableau. Absently she noticed papers and books strewn on the floor beside him, as if he had been working in bed before he slept.

His eyes went from black to green, and anger

blazed from them so hot all the words of argument died on her lips. Jalia shrank from his anger.

"Latif…"

"What the hell do you think you're doing?"

Desperately she sought for courage. "Why shouldn't I be here? I—"

"Get out!"

"It was all right for *you* to make love to me and try and break my resistance!" she pointed out hotly. "You have no right to react like an outraged virgin if I try to do the same!"

He flung the coverlet aside. He was naked, a fact which seemed to make no impression on him, but the golden light and shadow playing with his lean and hungry physique made the breath catch in Jalia's throat.

He grabbed her upper arm in a tight clasp and stood upright, drawing her inexorably with him. "Out!" he said again.

She lifted a hand to drag the heavy fall of hair off her face. "Latif! Can't we—"

Her jade eyes glistened, her full mouth trembled, with passionate tears. "Latif!" she cried. "I miss you so much! Can't you just—"

His hand tightened on her arm as he stooped again, to pick up her robe.

"Can't I what?" he growled savagely. "Forget that you belong to another man? Am I such a fool?"

Her perfume rose from the garment's silken folds, clouding his senses, and he cursed, like a man who does not know he is drunk till he stands up.

"Latif!" she begged again, and watched, her lips

parting, as his flesh responded urgently to the scent and the memory of the pleasure it promised.

"Damn you!" he said and, tossing the robe away, he stepped towards her, drew her against him, wrapped her in a ruthless embrace. His mouth found hers with savage impatience, and then she was falling, dragged down to heaven by his arms.

The hunger in his kiss made her senses swim, and his hands pressed her with the possessive strength that melted her. The heat of his thighs enveloped hers, his body hard and unforgiving as it crushed her.

He lifted his mouth from hers and kissed her neck, her throat, her shoulder, and Jalia moaned with hungry abandon, her fingers twining and luxuriating in the thick curls of his hair as he drew his head up and kissed her mouth again.

With a suddenness that made the breath rasp in her throat, his legs slipped between hers and jerked them wide, his hard body pressing against the million nerve ends that clustered there.

There was a wildness in him, a fury almost, that she had half sensed before, but that he had always kept under tight control; now it was unleashed.

"Love," he murmured, as if the word were torn from his deepest being. "My Beloved."

Her heart soared and sang, and she gave herself up to his fierce embrace with joy like a tidal wave.

He dragged, almost tore off the silk that covered her, till she was naked under his burning gaze. He ran his hand down her body, like a sculptor reminding himself of the lines of a statue he himself has carved, breast, waist, thigh, lost to everything except that she was here, in his bed. Then he drove into her, into that hot home that was his and his alone, over and over, while she moaned and cried out and pushed against him, seeking what he only could give her.

His hands and his body pushed her, pulled her, clasped her, in a ruthless pleasure-seeking that kept her in that intoxicating borderland between pleasure and pain, till she was lost to everything except the world of the senses.

He used all he had learned about her, and with every pleasure-drugged moment he taught her more. She hovered on the edge of blasting sensation for long, agonizing, thrilling seconds, crying and singing with its approach, and at last, with wild determination, he drove her over into ecstasy, and joined her there, so that they clung together as they soared, calling and crying, helplessly giving in to sensation, like two lovers who leap from a cliff.

Drenched with sweat then, he slipped down beside her, and Jalia turned with a grateful sigh to seek his embrace.

He sat up and gazed down at her in silence. She stared at him, seeing nothing but a dark shadow limned against the halo of light that surrounded him. His expression she could not discern.

But his tone of voice said it all.

"This changes nothing, Jalia."

It was like touching cold stone where you had expected living flesh.

"What?" she faltered.

"I play by your rules now. We make love, but it does not touch my heart. If you return to my bed another night, be sure to take no notice of anything I may say in the insanity of pleasure. It is meaningless."

Eighteen

"**O**f course I had no hand in it," Michael said. "Haven't you noticed that the gossip has never been picked up by the *Herald?* Ellin's livid about it."

"Ellin is?" Jalia exclaimed. "She's not the one being made to look a fool!"

"And what about me? Not that it's not totally deserved." Michael tossed down the paper, in which another columnist mauled the tasty story of the Princess's passion. "You're probably going to have to get used to it, Jalia. As I understand it, you should be grateful when what the papers say isn't true. It's when it's true it really bites."

"I suppose so."

Michael looked up, his mouth slowly falling open.

"Ah. My God, how thick I've been! Of course. It is true. That's why you're so bothered."

"No! At least, they're wrong in saying that's why I wanted the engagement. At that time I had no idea how I felt."

He snapped his fingers. "Latif was there at the airport, wasn't he? I should have seen it then, the way he was... But didn't he say he was your bodyguard?"

"You said it. He only agreed."

"Christ! You should have told me, Jalia! Why didn't you just tell me to get on my horse and—"

"Because you had Ellin Black right beside you, Michael."

He closed his eyes and shook his head. "From this moment I renounce champagne. But we've got to find a way out of this. Shall I talk to him? Would it help?"

Jalia shook her head, perilously near tears. "He knows, he just—doesn't care."

"You know, Jalia, now that Noor's home safe, does it really matter so much if Ellin prints some story about a forced marriage? It's what I said before, you know—as long as what they're saying is *not* true, you should be grateful."

"My parents don't deserve the humiliation. Michael. Not while they're still in England, anyway. Imagine what the media attention would be like! I just—I wish there were another way out. For your sake, too."

"Don't worry about me! You know I'm in discussions with the Sultana about old Hafzuddin's collection. If that comes off I'll consider it a fair trade. Anyway, I quite fancy the role of bruised, used, and castaway lover!" he said.

* * *

One of her main concerns now, whether Latif liked it or not, was to find some solution for the various problems facing the women of Sey-Shahin Valley. She had discussed their issues with the Sultan and Sultana, but there was only so far she could go without the Shahin's approval.

"Why are you bothering with this?" Latif said, on a day when she had cornered him in his office in the palace and insisted on talking to him about it. "These women aren't your concern."

"They don't seem to be yours, either, Latif!" she replied smartly. "These women came to me with their—"

"Because they made an assumption that proved wrong," he pointed out coldly. "My wife will be expected to concern herself with these problems. You are not."

"I am not going to be a slave to what is *expected!* Now, I have some practical suggestions and solutions to offer. When are you going to visit the valley again?"

He drew himself up with righteous indignation. "Is one of your suggestions that you should accompany me again?"

"Will you shut up and listen a moment?" She was nearly shouting. Oh, the Ice Maiden had lost her grip, for sure. Sometimes Jalia felt as if she'd spent her life half-asleep, dreaming she was a doe munching in a field, and had awakened to discover herself a tigress gnawing some animal's flesh.

"This could be important to a lot of people and you have no business standing in the way because of personal animosity to me!"

His face hardened, his mouth narrowed, and his eyes glinted with an emotion she could only guess at.

"I have no personal animosity, Princess. Fire away," he said stiffly.

"Thank you. Now, first of all, I've engaged legal advice, both here and in England, to try and sort out that one-sided contract that's tying up the carpet weavers.

"If we're successful, and it's still a big if, the women will need a new agent for their carpets. The Sultana and I have been talking, and we think what's needed—not just in Sey-Shahin, but throughout the country—is a tribal cooperative agent appointed by the palace.

"In other words, one body that will agent for any tribal group that needs representation in markets abroad. I'll be helping Dana set up a team over the next few months. It will take operating expenses only, no commission."

Latif sat watching her, his face a mask.

"We're tentatively calling it the Tribal Arts Co-operative."

"I see."

"With the Sultana publicly involved, it should go over a treat. We think we can produce our own catalogue and organize worldwide distribution. Gazi al Hamzeh will be advising us about publicity on a pro bono basis."

"Gazi al Hamzeh?" he repeated, frowning.

"Don't you know him? He's Prince Karim's Cup Companion, and the hottest press agent going. Dana says he's an absolute wizard at planting information so it gets reported as news, instead of sending out press releases, which get ignored. He organized Ash's press campaign before Ghasib fell.''

''I do know him.''

''Dana said you did. We're also thinking about a coffee table book of Marzuqi rugs—we're hoping to get a lot of the world's well-known women who own them to let themselves be photographed with their carpets, and give little interviews.''

''And why are you telling me?'' He hadn't budged an inch.

''Also a whole series of little cookbooks. If it goes over well, we'd make a complete set, one for each of the tribes. Not just recipes, but pictures of the women planting and picking and cooking, and the tribal area, and the food. Starting with Sey-Shahin Valley.''

''Why are you telling me, Jalia?'' he said again, with a curious intensity.

''Surely you've noticed you're the Shahin, Latif!''

His eyes burned her. ''And what are you, Jalia?''

For a moment her throat caught with hope, but his jaw was clenched and angry.

''At the moment, the Sultana's representative,'' she said.

''THE PRINCESS I LOVE!''
Forbidden Wedding Will Go Ahead!

The marriage of Cup Companion Sheikh Bari al Khalid and Princess Noor al Jawadi Durrani, which was dramatically halted in Bagestan last month when the bride and groom mysteriously disappeared, is on again, according to sources.

The truth behind the mystery of the wedding couple's flight, only minutes before the ceremony was due to begin, has at last come out. Sources close to the couple have revealed that the Princess and her fiancé fled because Sheikh Jabir al Khalid, the groom's grandfather, dramatically withdrew his permission and barred the union at the eleventh hour. The couple intended to undertake the ceremony elsewhere. But their plane was forced down in a storm, and the rest is history. The couple spent what would have been their honeymoon on an uninhabited island, surviving on turtle eggs.

Their disappearance, the search, the dramatic rescue, and the couple's continuing devotion have had no influence on the old Sheikh's decision, however.

Bari al Khalid will be forced to sacrifice his expected inheritance, consisting of vast property in Bagestan, in order to marry the woman he loves. The legacy will now probably go to a cousin.

"My wife and I will build a new legacy together," the handsome Cup Companion has been quoted as saying. The wedding is expected to take place next month.

"Isn't it brilliant?" Noor said excitedly. "Bari *said* Gazi was the man to sort it out. Talk about saving the brand from the burning!"

It was the best news Jalia had had since the rescue.

"Is it true that Bari won't inherit if he marries you, or is that—?"

"Not a penny! As if we care!" Noor laughed, and Jalia smiled. The changes to Noor went very deep. "I still get the ring, though," Noor said, flashing the brilliant diamond, "because that he inherited from his father. Not that I care, but it is gorgeous, isn't it? It'll be a constant reminder to me of what's not important in life."

"It is gorgeous," Jalia agreed.

"Oh, and did I mention that we love each other after all?"

"Only a few dozen times. Was this story Gazi al Hamzeh's idea? He seems to be an all-around genius."

"I think he and Bari cooked it up between them," Noor said jealously. "And you're saved, too, I hope you notice! Anything anyone now says about forced marriages is going to look pretty limp, with Bari actually being disinherited—and me so obviously thrilled, of course. Gazi says it's the first time he's ever sorted out two clients' problems with one story."

"What?"

Noor bit her lip, grinning. "It was him all along. Apparently, he's been on your case for ages!"

Jalia stared. "On my case?"

"Don't you get it? Gazi's the one who's been leaking all those stories about you having the hots for Latif!"

Nineteen

The sun was going from the garden, its deep golden light brushing the leaves, glinting from the long rows of arched glass.

It lingered on Latif Abd al Razzaq's black hair, brushing it with glowing fingers as he bent over his desk, working. Jalia thought foolishly, *Even the sun can't bear to leave him.*

She stepped through the open doorway from the courtyard, her bare feet silent on the tiles, and crossed to his desk. His fountain pen scratched across the document as she watched. Then her shadow fell within his line of vision, and he looked up.

They looked at each other for a long still moment; then, as if there had been no pause, Latif carefully lifted his hand and capped the pen. Each movement was precise, as if it were necessary to maintain complete control over every tiniest muscle.

"Was it you?" she asked softly.

With the flick of an eye he dismissed the assistant who entered just then from the corridor. The man moved a fist to his breast, bowed and silently disappeared again.

"Was it?"

"You will have to explain what you mean," Latif said, and Jalia dropped the paper with the latest gossip item about them in front of him. He picked it up and gazed at it.

"Did you enlist Gazi al Hamzeh's media manipulation machine to leak all those stories about me?"

Latif abruptly pushed back his chair and stood, and in spite of herself Jalia stepped back a pace.

"Of course I did." As if he had suddenly tired of the game, he tossed the paper down on his desk and moved to stand in the open doorway.

Outside, beyond the green branches of the trees, a breeze was playing with the fountain. The courtyard was beguiling at this hour, shaded and sweet with the perfume of flowers that did not dare to open in the harsh glare of noon.

It was a moment before the sense of his words sank in, so convinced had she been that he would deny all knowledge.

"You did?"

"The campaign has achieved its goal, hasn't it?"

"What was the goal, apart from humiliating me?"

He glanced at her, then out at the garden again. "Gazi was of the opinion that we had to make a preemptive strike. The story about a forced marriage had to be discredited before it ran. Gazi knows his business."

"And how has it achieved that goal?" she asked.

"Don't you know? Your fiancé and his tame reporter were overheard having a loud argument in the Sultan's Return Hotel this afternoon. She accused him of deliberately misleading her. She has booked a seat to London on the midnight flight."

"It's the first I've heard," she said.

Silence fell. He watched the shadows in the garden, his jaw tight.

At last he turned to face her.

"What do you want out of life, Jalia?"

She blinked and caught her lip between her teeth. A last stray beam of sunshine darted over the roof to catch a spray of water from the fountain and turn it into liquid fire.

Like the beam of hope that suddenly pierced her heart.

"You know what I want. You don't—"

"Tell me again."

"I want the life you offered me before. I want to make my home here, where my people are, where my heart is." She had to press her lips together to stop them trembling. She swallowed.

"I haven't told anyone yet, Latif, but...the Sultana has asked me—she's offered me a position as her Cup Companion. I've thought it over hard, and I'm going to accept it. I think it offers me the best opportunity to make the contribution I want to make.

"So I'll be moving to Bagestan, whether you love me or not. And I guess if you really don't, it'll have to be enough, knowing I'm doing what I can for the people and the country."

She looked up, but still he was silent, watching her with his green falcon's eyes.

"But I want more than that, Latif. I love you. I want you to love me, the way you once did. I want to marry you, and have your children, and give them Bagestan as their home."

A sob caught in her throat. "But you don't want that anymore."

He moved towards her and put his arms around her, and she felt the masculine heat of his hands against her back. Their warmth moved into her blood, her heart, her head, and she lifted her face to smile up at him.

"My Beloved," said Latif, "who has told you such a terrible lie?"

And then she was home, against his heart.

Later, they walked in the garden, where the night flowers tempted the moonlight with their heady perfume. His arm was around her, her head against his shoulder.

"I thought that you did not know your own heart, that you loved me and did not know it. I thought I could teach you the truth of your feelings for me."

She said, "You were right, but it was a long time before I could admit it to myself. Was that why you tricked me into going into the mountains with you? It was a trick, wasn't it? All that talk about Mansour's young son. I finally saw it."

Latif laughed. "There was no hope of teaching you anything if I could not be with you, and you had been very adept at avoiding me before the wedding."

"And my mother knew!" Jalia exclaimed. "She must have been in on it, or she wouldn't—"

"Your parents understood my feelings. When you left the country so suddenly after the Coronation I couldn't hide my reaction from them. They knew what I intended, and what you meant to me."

Jalia shook her head. "That thought only occurred to me way too late. I should have guessed why my mother was so cool about my travelling around with you. 'Tell them he's your husband!'" She mimicked her mother's advice. "I seem to have walked into every trap you set for me."

"Why not?" he said, kissing her softly. "I had already walked into yours."

"And then, just when you thought you had me where you wanted me…"

"Just as I had begun to hope I had succeeded in showing you your heart, Michael was there, claiming you."

The fountain splashed in the darkness and she put out her arm to catch the soft cool drops of water on her skin. Sensation shivered to her scalp, as if at the touch of his fingers.

"When Michael turned up, did you think I'd lied on our…that night when I told you the engagement was invented?"

"On our wedding night," he amended firmly, and wrapped his arm more securely around her. "At first, perhaps. I was so maddened with jealousy I did not know what I believed. But that you had put yourself beyond my reach, stealing from me the chance to show you how strong our love could be, was certain.

And I had to accept that that might be exactly what you intended.''

''But I was appalled when Michael turned up! Didn't you see that?''

''That might have been only your distress at the presence of the journalists. Otherwise, I could see no reason for you not to repudiate the engagement instantly.''

A heavy blossom drooped from a branch overhead, offering them its musky perfume as they passed. Its scent mirrored the sweetness she felt in her heart. Jalia smiled and sighed.

''So I decided to play the Western game after all,'' he continued. ''To pretend that I no longer wanted you, in the hopes that it would make you see what you wanted, in order to show you your choices, and make you fear the truth that doors may close when we do not go through them at the right time.''

''And all the time you had Gazi on the case.''

''I could see no easy way out of that engagement once it was made public,'' Latif said. ''The story of a forced marriage might have dogged us for a very long time, and I thought it would make you and your parents unhappy. Do you blame me for taking steps to protect our future together even when it seemed we might not have one?''

''N-o-o-o. Poor Michael, though. And I look—''

''Michael will be made happy by the Sultan's silver plates. And when we find the Sey-Shahin treasures, I am sure he will be delighted if we ask him to examine them.''

She laughed aloud. ''Oh, that'll sort Michael out,

all right. And what about me…was it necessary to make me look such a mad fool?''

He turned to face her. ''Who is not mad, who loves?'' he demanded roughly. ''I am insane for you, Jalia. From the moment I first saw you I have been wandering in the desert like Majnun dreaming of his Layla.''

''But you stopped loving me,'' Jalia murmured. ''When I told you I loved you, you weren't even interested. I was too late. I'd left it too late. All of a sudden, you didn't care anymore.''

She looked up at him, her eyes shadowed with the memory of that dark moment.

''You had learned that you loved me. But you hadn't yet learned that you loved this country. How I wanted to take what you offered, what I had prayed for! But I knew it was a dangerous temptation. What would I do with a wife half-won, only grudgingly mine?'' He spoke as if he were understanding it clearly only as he spoke.

''I saw that if out of love for me you gave in grudgingly to the necessity to live here, we would never be truly happy.

''Life will not always be easy for us, Jalia. There is work ahead. I saw that if you did not come to me from a complete conviction that your home was here in Bagestan, there would be too much room for regret. You had to find your love for the country, too.''

She heaved a deep sigh for the old life—her friends, her students, the university. But she had no doubts anymore. Her life was here, her heart was here, her fate was to be beside Latif all her days.

"So I offered you scope to learn about your heart, and your blood, and your generosity."

"What do you mean?"

"Was it not partly your concern for the women of Sey-Shahin Valley that taught you that your heart was here in Bagestan?"

"Maybe," Jalia began indignantly, "but you can hardly take the credit for that! Offered me scope? If you suggested that I'm marrying you because otherwise the women of your valley won't get a look-in, you'd be closer..." Jalia's voice faded off as the last piece fell into place.

"Oh no! Oh, what an idiot I've been!"

He was laughing and shaking his head. "Did you really imagine, my Beloved, that I could care so little about something so important affecting my people's well-being, simply because it concerned women?"

"You set me up!" she accused. "Right from the start! Right from that day in Sey-Shahin!"

"I only feigned a little indifference in the hopes of engaging your interest on my people's behalf. I hoped that even if you did not love me, Jalia, your love of my people would teach you to love their Shahin."

"Or vice versa," said the Princess, and nestled against his heart.

Epilogue

PRINCESS WINS HER SHEIKH

Princess Jalia al Jawadi Shahbazi, recently appointed Cup Companion to the Sultana of Bagestan, and the Sultan's Cup Companion Latif Abd al Razzaq Shahin are to marry. A palace spokesman said that the possibility of a joint wedding with the Princess's cousin, Noor, and her fiancé, Bari al Khalid, has not been ruled out.

* * * * *

Look for Alexandra Sellers's next
SONS OF THE DESERT *title,*
THE FIERCE AND TENDER SHEIKH, in
January 2005, only in Silhouette Desire.

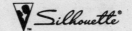

introduces an exciting new family saga
with

DYNASTIES: THE DANFORTHS

A family of prominence...
tested by scandal, sustained by passion!

THE CINDERELLA SCANDAL by Barbara McCauley
(Silhouette Desire #1555, available January 2004)

MAN BENEATH THE UNIFORM by Maureen Child
(Silhouette Desire #1561, available February 2004)

SIN CITY WEDDING by Katherine Garbera
(Silhouette Desire #1567, available March 2004)

SCANDAL BETWEEN THE SHEETS by Brenda Jackson
(Silhouette Desire #1573, available April 2004)

THE BOSS MAN'S FORTUNE by Kathryn Jensen
(Silhouette Desire #1579, available May 2004)

CHALLENGED BY THE SHEIKH by Kristi Gold
(Silhouette Desire #1585, available June 2004)

COWBOY CRESCENDO by Cathleen Galitz
(Silhouette Desire #1591, available July 2004)

STEAMY SAVANNAH NIGHTS by Sheri WhiteFeather
(Silhouette Desire #1597, available August 2004)

THE ENEMY'S DAUGHTER by Anne Marie Winston
(Silhouette Desire #1603, available September 2004)

LAWS OF PASSION by Linda Conrad
(Silhouette Desire #1609, available October 2004)

TERMS OF SURRENDER by Shirley Rogers
(Silhouette Desire #1615, available November 2004)

SHOCKING THE SENATOR by Leanne Banks
(Silhouette Desire #1621, available December 2004)

Available at your favorite retail outlet.

If you enjoyed what you just read,
then we've got an offer you can't resist!

Take 2 bestselling love stories FREE!

Plus get a FREE surprise gift!

Coming in January 2005

BETWEEN MIDNIGHT AND MORNING
by Cindy Gerard
Silhouette Desire #1630

Small-town veterinarian Alison Samuels hardly expected to start a fiery affair with hunky young rancher John Tyler. To John, she was a stimulating challenge, and Alison was more than game. But he hid a dark past, and Alison wasn't one for surprises....

Available wherever Silhouette books are sold.

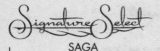

COMING NEXT MONTH

#1627 ENTANGLED—Eileen Wilks
Dynasties: The Ashtons
Years ago, Cole Ashton and Dixie McCord's passionate affair had ended when Cole's struggling business had taken priority over Dixie. Now, she was back in his life and Cole hoped for a second chance. But even if he could win Dixie once more, would Cole be able to make the right choice this time?

#1628 HER PASSIONATE PLAN B—Dixie Browning
Divas Who Dish
Spunky nurse Daisy Hunter never thought she'd find the man of her dreams while on the job! But when a patient's relative, athlete Kell McGee, arrived in town, she suddenly had to make a difficult decision—stick to her old agenda for finding a man or switch to passionate Plan B!

#1629 THE FIERCE AND TENDER SHEIKH—Alexandra Sellers
Sons of the Desert
Sheikh Sharif found long-lost Princess Shakira fifteen years after she'd escaped her family's assassination. As the beautiful princess helped heal her homeland, Sharif passionately worked on mending Shakira's spirit. Though years as a refugee had left her hardened, could the fierce and tender sheikh provide the heat needed to melt Shakira's cool facade and expose her heart?

#1630 BETWEEN MIDNIGHT AND MORNING—Cindy Gerard
When veterinarian Alison Samuels moved into middle-of-nowhere Montana, she hardly expected to start a fiery affair, especially with hunky young rancher John Tyler. To J.T., this tantalizing older woman was a stimulating challenge and Alison was more than game. But J.T. hid a dark past and Alison wasn't one for surprises....

#1631 IN FORBIDDEN TERRITORY—Shawna Delacorte
Playboy Tyler Farrel was totally taken when he laid eyes on the breathtakingly beautiful Angie Coleman. She was all grown up! Despite their mutual attraction, Ty wouldn't risk seducing his best friend's kid sister until Angie, sick of being overprotected, decided to step into forbidden territory.

#1632 BUSINESS AFFAIRS—Shirley Rogers
When Jenn Cardon placed the highest bid at a bachelor auction, she had no idea she'd just landed a romantic getaway with sexy blue-eyed CEO Alex Dunnigan—her boss! Thanks to cozy quarters, sexual tension turned into unbridled passion. Alex wasn't into commitment but Jenn had a secret that could keep him around...forever.

SDCNM1204